Rutland Quincy Sherwood's Unbelievable Guide to Salvaging the Impossible

A novel by Daniel Reed

05/01/2018
Rutland Quincy Sherwoods Unbelievable Guide to Salvaging the Impossible
Written and Edited by: Daniel Alexander Reed
Do nothing from selfish ambition or conceit but in humility count others more significant than yourselves.
Philippians 2:3
@TheFindersKeep

For my Dearest Amos... the one who finds joy at every turn.

- All my love, Dad
Never Perfect. Always Better.

Chapter 1

Rutland Quincy Sherwood was by no means a man of simple truths or small adventures, no, rather he was a man of gaping wide mystery with enough secrets that would take all of eternity to uncover. As that is the amount of time it will take me to make sense of his 'Unbelievable Guide to Salvaging the Impossible'.

Rutland may not be with us here but every night before I go to bed I look upon the stars and pray that he is out there salvaging to the fullest extent of his heart. His soul wish was for me to always find happiness in my career and that is why I have given one hundred percent control of the firm to my dad Brunley who has hired quite nicely in the last few months or so, given him and my mum some time to travel.

As much as I enjoyed the practice of the law and the balance it brings to society, it was time for me to get into the real family business of salvaging. I have spent the better half of the last six months reading through his extensive notes as Holly and Eliza helped Duncan get acquainted with life in London while simultaneously planning our fall wedding which is the best compromise we could come up with as she wanted summer and I enjoy the brisk calm air of winter, why not just split the difference.

To be honest if you asked me a year ago where do you see yourself a year from now, married was certainly not in the deck of cards but as Rutland always believed, when you know something to be true, pursue it at all cost.

RING! RING! The phone rang blaringly from beneath the pile of notebooks, maps and drawings as I frantically searched for it before answering. "Sherwood Salvaging, the stranger the acquisition in need the better the keep, this is Arthur speaking. How may I help you find your way today?"

"Arthur Sherwood is that really you?" The elderly lady from across the street called about once a week with something for me to find.

"Yes Mrs. Garrison it would be I, Arthur!"

"It seems I have lost my late husband's favorite watch and I just cannot sleep without knowing its whereabouts." She screeched.

"Alright now, calm down, I am sure it's around somewhere, I will be over in a few minutes." I made myself presentable for the job which she always paid for promptly and though it wasn't an exciting salvage, she happened to be our number one customer. I rang the knocker and waited for her to come to the door.

"Arthur come on in my dear, thank you for coming on such short notice and quickly I might add." She was wearing her favorite pink bathrobe and comfy slippers, glasses slightly tilted at the edge of her nose and her cane in hand.

"Anytime Ms. Garrison, you are our number one customer after all!" I reassured her, as sad as it sounded. "So what does this watch actually look like?"

"It is gold with a minute an hour and a second hand on the face. It has his initials on the back and a diamond in the center of the watch. The numbers are roman numerals and I believe it has the letters TM on it."

"Are you pulling one on me, your husband owned a watch made by Thomas Mercer. We most certainly will find it and after we find it please lock it up in a safe place as I am sure it is a one of kind timepiece."

We started our search in her cellar going through box after box after box of fascinating truly extraordinary objects that I am sure have a story or two to go with them. "Well it certainly isn't down here and as much as I have enjoyed rummaging through the cellar, is there another possible place it might be?"

"He always spent a lot of time in his garage. Maybe we might have a look out there?" She slowly led the way.

We moved through the tools on the shelf and into the work bench until it was time to pull the cover off of the car. It was more than likely that we would not find the watch in the car but I had to know what was under the cover. The dust settled and there before my very eyes was a 1925 Aston Martin Twin Cam Grand Prix. "Did he restore this himself?"

"Restore it, no need to when he has taken care of it all these years, everything you see there was original assembly!"

"She is beautiful, does she still run?"

"She hasn't been taken out in months, maybe if you wash it you and Eliza can ride off in it on your wedding day!"

"Really? That would be amazing but first let's find that watch. Do you have the time by any chance?" As soon as those words left my mouth she pulled the watch out of her robe pocket without even thinking.

"Oh well my dear, would you look at that you found his watch, and just in time too."

"In time for what?"

"Here you go!" She handed me a hundred

pounds per our agreed upon payment. "Don't spend it all in one place."

"This really isn't necessary!" I tried to hand it back but she pushed me out the door.

As I crossed the street there she was staring intently at me through her window. She was like a cat lady without cats, which was stranger than if she actually were to have cats. Nice enough though I walked through the front door and into a surprise stag party.

"Surprise!!!" Duncan and Holly had planned me a pre-wedding gathering of sorts.

"Come on the guests are to be arriving soon. We just figured since Eliza got a bridal shower, we would invite a few of your friends and by your friends I mean all of my friends." Holly concluded as Eliza was humming from the kitchen preparing the meal.

"So Ms. Garrison was just a setup, a ploy?"

"Well she was supposed to keep you away longer at least until the guests all arrived but that plan obviously went out the window."

"Oh how lovely you used a poor old lady as a pawn in your game of surprise which I must say thank you, but really you didn't have to go through all the trouble."

"It was no trouble at all, really Arthur, I mean yes to actually get someone to show up on your behalf was a large task but I believe your old pal Struthers will be along any time now."

"Struthers? You mean the boy who made my childhood a living nightmare!"

"Oops I mean he said you two were like best friends back in the day. I use to always see you sitting together at lunch."

"That was because if I didn't give him my lunch he would torture me. Still haven't gotten all of the toilet water out of my ear from his swirlies."

"Oh alright then, what about Andrew Molart from your old law firm? He will be here too."

"Yeah can't say I even know who that is." I could see that they tried their best but it wasn't really their fault as I kept to myself mostly.

"Look you all are here and for me that is plenty enough cheer for this night to be perfect."

My parents' car pulled up the drive. "And what exactly is my dad doing here?"

Eliza poked her head in the living room. "I have not the slightest clue, Holly did you invite him?"

"I most certainly did not."

Duncan put his hand up. "Yes Duncan, you do not need to raise your hand to speak."

"I invited him as it is a custom of Findas for the father to see off his son properly before his wedding. Have I overstepped?"

"No it is quite alright, but best to leave any mentioning of Findas out of tonight's festivities and let's leave the toasting up to my dad and Holly." I nodded to him.

The night grew louder as the room filled up and closed in on us as Holly knew just about half of London it seemed.

"Arthur Sherwood! How are you mate?" This big galoot of a man strung me up from behind nearly cracking every bone in my body.

"Brock Struthers, so nice of you to join us on this occasion. What have you been up to?"

"Well I just got out of the lock last week and my psychiatrist said I need to deal with my anger issues by asking for forgiveness for those I may have caused harm to."

"So here you are?"

"Well Arthur I picked on you quite a bit as we were growing up, and I guess I tricked your cousin into thinking we were friends so that I could apologize in person to you."

"Well my dear boy, it is water under the bridge! Now could you put me down?"

"Oh right sorry, sometimes I forget my manners but only sometimes anymore. Prison changes a man you know."

"No I don't but I guess a small cell with cold bars will make anyone think on their regrets."

"Oh no, mine was pretty big with white padded walls. I am just considered an outpatient now but we refer to it as a prison because off my meds it can feel that way sometimes."

"Right you are, please do excuse me and

enjoy the rest of the party."

I pulled Holly aside. "Do you realize that Struthers is a mental patient at the local looney bin?"

"No I could have sworn he was wearing a doctor's coat when I saw him."

"Nope that was his hospital gown I would assume."

"Ohhh fiddles, honest mistake?" She shrugged.

"Okay just make sure he leaves sooner than later as I do not want to cause a scene in front of our guests."

Aside from a few awkward encounters that night and my memory remaining intact I would say everything was going swimmingly up until the toasts were about to be made.

"Alright everyone gather around, and please turn your attention to the screen." My father brought over our family photo projector.

"The first photo I have for you all, is Arthur's first steps and this right here is the door he walked into right after the photo was taken."

"Arthur, you were such a cute kid." Eliza laughed. "Are we sure that's Arthur in these photos?"

"And here he is with his cousin Holly on Easter at Rutland's house."

"He always hosted the biggest egg hunts in this house."

"You know Arthur no matter how old you get you will always be my little Wubsie."

"And that's the end of the show lets hear it for my dad Brunley everyone." I cut in before he could continue any further down memory lane.

"Hold on I want to hear about Wubsie!" Eliza grabbed my hand.

"It is nothing really, when I was younger I couldn't say mummy properly so when I would get cranky everything sounded like WUBSIE! WUBSIE!" I even did an impersonation so that we could move on as quickly as possible.

"That is pure gold, that is. This has been a most informative time." Eliza was very pleased with all of the reminiscing.

"Everyone put your glass in the air as we toast to the bachelor, now I know I am newest to you all but I would take a sword to the heart for that man right there. I mean I would go to war for him if he asked." We gave him the look of let's move on to a different topic. "Oh right, right when I first met Arthur he was how do you say more brains then bronze. Heart of gold he has. He went from lawyer to Dra'kon rider."

"Alright it would appear Duncan has gone off the deep end. Dra'kon rider is a salvaging term by the way and with that a shameless plug for our new business. Here is to finding that which is lost and returning it from once where it came."

"Cheers!"

The evening lasted for another few hours before we cleaned up and headed off to bed. Eliza got to enjoy the comfort of our brand new king size bed in our fully furnished master bedroom, while I enjoyed my last nights a bachelor on the comfy couch we added to Rutland's thinking room right in front of his painting. I couldn't help but always feel like the painting was staring at me which made it tough to sleep the last week. Oh, and then there is always Duncan's snoring from down the hall. He sounded like he was cutting trees down in the Shadoway forest.

Right as I nodded off, Holly interrupted my peaceful rest. I turned on the lamp next to the couch. "Holly what seems to be the bother?"

"I can't seem to find my way through the nightmares anymore. All I keep seeing is Lachlan's face over and over, night after night I can hear his last breath."

"Aww Holly my dear it will be alright, you did all you could, and it is important to know that Lachlan embraced death as he did life, with honor. He was a true Keeper of Findas."

"All of that death didn't bother you?" she whimpered.

"I honestly cannot get Rutland out of my mind. Can I show you something?"

"Sure anything at all!"

I led her down the hall to my current office

and opened the desk drawer. I handed her the bottle of ink as she stared at me like a lunatic.

"You wanted to show me an ink bottle?"

"Oh right, yes well this isn't just any ink bottle. I brought this exact bottle to Findas and gave it to Rutland myself. I saw him get sucked into that sphere of light myself and there is no way he survived."

"And you are sure that he had the bottle of ink on him at the time?"

"I am most certain of it!"

"Well then I think you have your answer, Rutland's ghost has come back to haunt us."

"Very funny Holly!" I could tell she didn't believe me.

"Isn't it obvious to you that he clearly survived whatever it was that happened in there and clearly is now wherever he is but went out of his way to let you know he is ok. You should be thrilled."

"Why not just come back to us?"

"Because it is never that simple with Rutland. Does anyone else know about this?"

"No honestly I haven't thought to tell Eliza because I am afraid she will think I am a loon."

"Well probably best not to keep a secret from her and if anyone would understand; your, soon to be wife, will for sure." She comforted me.

"Now let's try and get some sleep yeah?"

"Sounds good to me! Can I crash on the

couch like old times?" She grabbed a pillow and blanket and laid down the opposite end of the couch from me.

The sun came blazing into the room as Eliza stood at the curtain. "Come on you two! Time to get up, no time to waste. Mum Sherwood will be here any minute to go over the last details for Saturday."

We rushed to get ready as Eliza went back into the kitchen to finish fixing breakfast as it was her favorite meal in the day to prepare. "And Arthur you have five minutes, not an hour please be ready in a jiff."

"Thanks for the inspiration love."

"Make that three minutes, your mum just pulled up the drive. Duncan, please come set the table!"

My mum came up to the side entrance by the kitchen. "It is open Mrs. Sherwood, come on in."

She entered in like a hurricane. "Is Arthur around?"

"He is in the shower."

"Perfect, drop what you are doing and come with me." My mum dragged her away from the stove and up the stairs to try on her wedding dress. She held it up for a brief moment then went behind her changing partition and made her grand entrance.

"Just as I thought!" My mum said to her.

"And what are you thinking?"

"Simply gorgeous!" They had a moment just the two of them before Holly walked in and screamed so loud it peaked my interest.

"Is everything alright ladies?"

"Yes, we are fine Arthur, now go away you mustn't see the bride in her dress before the wedding."

"Can someone come help me with this please?" Duncan yelled from the kitchen.

I ran quickly to his aid as smoke was flowing into the living room, we opened the windows and turned on every fan we could find. "What happened to the bacon?"

"Well I thought I turned the stove off but I accidentally turned it on high and then the grease splattered and smoke was everywhere, so I tossed some of the powder from the closet onto it as we used a similar substance to stop Agnar's fire raids."

"Well looks like we will be having coffee and biscuits. No worries maybe grab some berries from the fridge and the whipped cream. Also my mum is here so let's keep the magical land talk to a dull roar." We set the rest of the breakfast out on the table and waited for the girls to come down.

"So I have been thinking." Duncan paused.

"Go on mate."

"I have been thinking of asking Holly to be

my wife."

"That's fantastic news she will be thrilled."

"I was just wondering if there were any customs I should be aware of before asking her."

"Well usually you have to ask her parents for their permission and then you have to go pick out a ring that will symbolize your love to her forever. Then you need to come up with an elaborate plan to surprise her with the question."

"And you did this all for Eliza?"

"Well not quite all of it but yes we did sort of, it is actually a funny story for another time."

"And how did you two manage to ruin breakfast?"

"Hi Mum!"

"Hi Mrs. Sherwood."

"Duncan always a pleasure." My mum greeted him as they found their seats. "Now as Arthur's best man you will need to keep him in check so that Eliza can have the wedding of her dreams. Because Saturday is all about the bride."

"Got it, consider it done."

"And Holly you will need to make sure that Eliza is completely taken care of. So please take her to a ladies day at the salon, maybe a mud bath yeah."

"Don't need to tell me twice."

"Finally Arthur and Eliza, please make sure that there are no surprises of any kind the day of the wedding as I am sure you know this cost your father and I, a small fortune."

"I cannot make any promises!" I said cheekily as she walked out the front door.

Completely by own admission I only had one surprise in mind, when everyone headed off to bed I found myself going behind Old Merlin's door to bring back some extra guests for the wedding.

Behind the door was all of the same sense of adventure just a little more order as Holly and I organized the room from top to bottom.

"Right where I left you." I picked up the sword and struck the stone hard landing myself in the throne room of Queen Evelyn.

"Arthur, what took you so long?" I was greeted with warm delight as I prepped Finlay, Althia and Evelyn for the festivities ahead of us.

"Alright you three as far as anyone is concerned, Eve, you are Eliza's Aunt and Finlay her cousin and obviously Althia, you are Finlay's wife so that should be easy enough to remember. I can see you got the clothes I left for you."

"I made a few alterations to mine, I hope you don't mind." Finlay showed me the throwing ax he had tucked on the inside of his jacket pocket.

"Woah, what is it with every Keeper needing to carry a weapon at all times?"

"A Keeper should never be without…"

"I know but in London it is not customary to carry weapons as fashionably accessible as you've made it."

"Alright, alright Arthur. I will leave it here."

"Perfect now when we get to the house you must remain extra quiet. I set a place for everyone to sleep until we surprise Eliza in the morning."

"We completely understand. Now if you would be so kind as to lead the way." The queen handed me a sword and one by one we made our way back to Rutland's estate.

Chapter 2

The day has come for a celebration that would be short lived as it were. The wedding itself went off without a hitch but you see nothing was ever normal with my family. The church was perfectly staged for our liking, we had a stand in reverend as the one who had performed Rutland's funeral apparently vanished on a sabbatical. My parents invited family from all over so sneaking a few guests from Findas was the least of my worries.

"Mum!" Eliza was quite surprised as she walked into my room to find some familiar faces. "Finlay! Althia it is most wonderful to see you. But how did you, Arthur!" she yelled my name in excitement.

"Yes dear!"

She pulled aside. "Your mother specifically said no surprises and as much as I am floored with the gesture, this might have been a proper discussion?"

"Well I know but my parents invited like everyone we know so I figure I would give them clothes to blend in and do something nice for you."

"You really are quite the charmer, Mr. Sherwood."

"I am, and since they are here now, there is no need to be sending them back, if anyone asks. Eve is your Aunt and Finlay is your cousin and Althia his wife. Now Duncan and I will meet you all at the church and as long as everything goes as planned they will be back to Findas and we will be off on our honeymoon by morning."

Duncan and I headed over to pick up the car from Mrs. Garrison and off to the church we went. There was a portly man short in stature with a slight slouch in his shoulder standing on the step of the church.

"Excuse me kind sir." He held up his hand as I approached. "Are you the man I am looking for?"

"Well that depends, who is it that you are

looking for?"

"The owner of Sherwood Salvaging my good man, Arthur Sherwood."

"And if I was or knew of him, who should I say was asking for him?"

"The name is Chadwick von Winkler, a friend of a friend as it were and I am in need of your expertise in the field of acquiring rare items. As this mutual friend of ours is in need of our assistance most immediately."

"And this mutual friend of ours is a close one?" I pulled out my business card to hand to him. "For what it is worth, I am Arthur and I will be out of the office until next week as today I am getting married."

"I am sorry but I do not think we have that long and yes you will be quite surprised as to how close we three are."

"Well sir I am sorry but whatever it is you are looking for will have to wait until we get back."

"Right you are! Forgive me for any lack of proper manner." He tipped his hat and walked down to the lot to get in his car.

"Arthur who is… was that?" I turned around to my mother who was an earthquake of emotion on such a day as this. "Eliza is on her way with her Aunt and Cousin by the way. Thank you for the heads up, I had to redo all the seating charts to fit them in."

"Mum it will be just fine, he was nobody too important a potential client and plus didn't you want to meet some of her family?"

"You are right! I am just so stressed out and want this day to be perfect for you."

"Mum, I have Eliza and that is all I need for this day to be perfect. You doing all this for us is more than we could ever ask for. Actually it is way more than we asked for."

"I know, just want the best for my Arthur is all. Now get your butt inside, you cannot be seeing the bride with her dress before she makes her way down the aisle."

The rest of the day was a complete blur as I shook more hands than I had friends and family members, my mum even invited the nurse who delivered me, not to mention my ex-girlfriend who I hadn't seen since law school. We finally made it through our front door in peace and quiet as the cheers had worn off and the inevitable post celebration meal was waiting for us in the fridge as neither of us could remember eating.

"Kind of quiet here without Duncan and Holly don't you think?"

"It is but they promised to show your mum and the other two a good time in the city so that we could have some time to ourselves, alone." I winked at her as soon as I knew it the door bell was ringing.

"Are you blooming joking me, who could

possibly be at the door at this hour on our wedding night?" Eliza wondered aloud as I reluctantly opened the peep hole as the man on the other side continued to buzz the doorbell.

"Can I help you?" He stormed right passed me and into the living room. "Mr. von Winkler what do I owe the pleasure and what part of I won't be back to the office until next week did you misunderstand?"

"Yes I certainly do apologize Arthur but this could wait no longer. Are we alone?"

"No my wife who is also part owner of the salvaging company who also won't be in the office until next week, is in the other room."

"Oh right well invite her in, she should hear this as well." He huffed.

"Arthur who was it?" She waltzed into the room. "I mean is it?"

"The name is Chadwick von Winkler and I am in need of your service, I will pay you whatever you wish and all expedition costs will also be taken care of."

"One moment please." I pulled Eliza aside as she cut me off.

"We will take the job and go on our holiday after, we really need the work. He also stated that we get to name our own price."

"You sure?" I asked her knowing that whatever we were about to go in search of would most likely be more exciting than a week in my parents house by the beach.

"Before we go any further Mr. von Winkler. What is it that you are in need of acquiring?"

"Just call me Chadwick please and it's not so much a what, but rather a, whom. I am sure there will be many what's to find along the way but ultimately I need you to find an old friend of mine."

"I am not sure you understand what we do here. We find artwork, sculptures, ancient civilizations, shipwrecks and things thought lost to this world. But people is not one of the things we acquire."

"What about things lost to other worlds, people lost to other worlds?" He perched up knowingly.

"I have not the slightest clue of what you are talking about sir. But out of curiosity who is it that you are in search of?"

"Finally a question worth more questions I am sure. Our mutual friend is the one I seek, the incredible Mr. Rutland Quincy Sherwood of course."

"I am sorry to tell you this but my uncle Rutland passed away six months ago."

"That is not possible, I was with him two weeks ago in that very church I was standing in front of today."

"You are a close friend you say, but I don't remember seeing you at the funeral though."

"It would seem you didn't remember seeing your own uncle there either because we both know that whatever was in that hideous vase was not the incredible Rutland Quincy Sherwood."

"I beg your pardon."

"Your uncle owns that old church, do I need to spell it out for you."

I closed my eyes thought back as hard as I possibly could and underneath that beard and suit was that familiar smile I couldn't believe I had let slip past me. "Oh my goodness you mean Rutland was the reverend at his own funeral."

"Now you are on to something my boy."

"What are you saying Arthur?" Eliza nosed her way in. "Rutland is alive?"

"It is possible and actually explains a lot more than it would seem to confuse. Well I know I should have shown you this sooner." I grabbed the ink bottle and placed it in her hands. "I brought this to Findas with me and gave it to Rutland. I found it back in the desk drawer I got it from."

"I am sorry I don't mean to pry but you have been to Findas?" He looked at us with genuine interest. "What was it like?"

"Well outside of the ongoing war it was a quite beautiful place, and just how do you know about Findas?"

"That my boy is a conversation for another day but now we must head back to the church."

"I am sorry but what is at the church."

"The first clues to finding Rutland. You know he told me you were the brains out of you and him."

"Oh my kind sir, believe me I am, but as you can imagine this all is a lot to process."

"No worries you can process the rest on the way over. I will drive to save us time." He had a lead foot as he did not once go under the speed limit. "And we are here."

"I think I am going to be sick." Eliza threw up outside of the car. "Do you really need to drive like such a lunatic?"

"My sincere apologies but time is not currently on our side and given our present circumstance, there is more than you know at stake here."

"Well maybe if we had a better idea of what you were so hurried about maybe we could be of better service. Also, is now a bad time to go over our fee?"

"We are looking for the Last Hymn of the Psalmist Council. Your uncle could play it from memory, I unfortunately was not gifted when it came to the theory of music."

"Sounds easy enough an old church loaded with hymnals, how hard could it be to scroll through and find one hymn." Eliza declared the salvage to begin.

"Also I transferred three million pounds

into your account shortly after meeting you outside of the church."

"But what if we said no."

"But you didn't now did you?"

"Fair enough." I was in no position to argue.

"The specific piece of music we are looking for was written in concordance with the original Amazing Grace it is said that the notes can be found within the song itself but it would take many lifetimes to get the combination just right."

"So we need the original sheet music?"

"Last I heard Rutland had found it on one of his many voyages and that it is somewhere in this church."

This was par for the course with Rutland, that even on my wedding night I found myself ready to break into a church which he just so happened to own to find an object he had acquired some time ago which is now probably hidden very well in the most unlikely of places.

"Almost got it, one more turn and voila! We are in." I pushed the door open slowly.

"His office is right off to the side of the sanctuary."

"That is a brilliant place to start, I will lead the way since you both seem to have forgotten one important thing, a light to see." Eliza pulled her flashlight from her purse.

"Right you are, lead the way my dear."

The floorboards creaked beneath our footsteps as we entered into the room. Chadwick turned on the light at yet another one of Rutland's desks. Eliza scoured the books on the shelf for almost an hour but was unsuccessful in her findings. I tried every knob removed every painting and looked under every pew while Chadwick sat ever so comfortably in Rutland's office.

"I don't understand a document of that importance he most certainly kept it close to him." Chadwick pitched us his two cents.

"Well it would seem that it is not here."

"Hold on to that next statement, take a look at this." Eliza pointed at the wall behind Chadwick.

"And exactly what am I looking at?"

"This wall is not like the others. It only appears to be."

"Are you seeing things? It's the same exact wall paper as the others."

She grabbed the letter opener from the desk and ran the blade in the corner at the bottom where the wall met the floor. She started to tear the paper from the wall.

"Would you look at that? He hid them in the walls. How did you even spot that?"

"I noticed that the paper on this wall seemed thicker than the rest and then I just hoped I wasn't wrong." She laughed.

"Let's call it a night and make sense of this

in the morning, shall we?" We hurried along as it was getting late.

"I will be staying at the local Inn down the road. I will see you two tomorrow morning."

He dropped us off and sped away. We were met with a loud crash as we entered the home. To our surprise we found Duncan, Holly and the others having a grand old time.

"What are you doing here?" I demanded.

"I am sorry but the real question my good man is what were you two not doing here?" Finlay and Duncan had pillows in hand and ties around their heads with the dress shirts I gave them untucked.

"Holly, a word please." We stepped into the kitchen. "And just what are the five of you doing back here, as you were given specific instructions to be out of sight until the morning."

"Yeah well plans sort of changed as the hotel flooded, which I am not saying we had something to do with it but I am not saying we didn't indirectly cause it."

"Perfect and now you are fugitives."

"Not technically but anyway enough about our night, where did you two go off to?"

"As it were we have been offered an expedition of sorts, by a man who carries more secrets than maybe even Rutland himself."

"Did you take the offer?"

"Yes we did accept his offer."

"For what and how much?"

"Three million pounds, but the tricky part is the acquisition itself."

She looked completely flabbergasted by the proposition of the generous amount we had been given. "And the acquisition is quite rare or of some sort extreme value?"

"Try impossible, the man is asking us to find Rutland."

"What about Rutland?" Evelyn smitten at the sound of his name, danced into the kitchen.

"Alright everyone in the living room now, Eliza please get our guests some water, as it would seem they are a bit parched."

"Arthur don't be such a downer mate." Duncan snickered. "We were only having a bit of fun."

"As much as pillow boxing sounds like a jolly time. We have some business to attend to before we call it a night."

They all looked at me with joyful smiles. "Well let's hear you out now."

"A man by the name of Sir Chadwick von Winkler has bestowed upon us a quest of sorts and since it involves a man we all love, I figure it is best that I give everyone a chance to have a say."

"I don't understand how this von Winkler knows someone we all are acquainted with."

"He wants us to find Rutland and says it is

time sensitive."

"He is alive?" Evelyn gasped.

"From what von Winkler has told us he disappeared two weeks ago and he fears the longer he is missing the smaller the chance of us finding him at all."

"I am most definitely in." Duncan raised his hand like usual.

"Evelyn I know this is a lot to take in but if you are not up for this I completely understand."

"Nonsense, Finlay and Althia will go back to Findas and make sure the kingdom is taken care of. I will go with you all to save Rutland as he has saved me a time or two." She seemed eager.

"We will go at once my Queen." Finlay and Althia left for Findas as we all unraveled into our dreams.

Chapter 3

I arose particularly early as the dreams I hoped for were interrupted by memories of Rutland. I grabbed my robe from the closet door and went down stairs to start a brew of my favorite thinking juice. I stumbled around the kitchen to find Evelyn sitting at the table.

"Having trouble sleeping too?"

"Arthur don't you know it is rude to sneak up on someone like that."

"I am sorry Eve, I don't mean to frighten you, I just couldn't sleep. I have been reliving that day in Findas over and over night after night for months now."

"I know the feeling. You wouldn't happen to have any coffee would you?"

"I am just about to make some and start in on this sheet music."

"Well I won't be much help with the music but I can drink a pot of coffee or two."

"You know about coffee?"

"Oh yes, I am how you say a connoisseur, as it was one of the only items from this world I allowed into Findas. Rutland introduced it to us on one of his many adventures. The aroma alone lifts my spirits."

I began to hum the melody softly as reading from the hand written staffs of John Newton was truly electrifying. I noticed Eve humming with me.

"You know this tune?"

"Oh yes I am quite familiar, Rutland use to hum it quite often, never the words only the melody."

"It would seem that this may just be a dead end."

"The one thing I know about Rutland is that it is never what it seems and too often its different then what it actually appears to be. It is never a dead end but usually an alternate route." I held the sheet music up as the sun burst through the window over the sink. Notes appeared that were not originally on the staff. I moved it away from the light and they were gone.

"You Eve are a truly magnificent being maybe even a little more layered then even Rutland himself."

I started to transpose the missing notes onto their own staff in order as they appeared within the music. In another life I may have truly pursued my love of music but for now it was a hobby that came quite in handy at dinner parties mostly and as of now in the field of salvaging.

"Does everything come this naturally for all you Sherwood's?"

"Well no not particularly, in this case my mum insisted on me playing the piano from an early age and my dad always said that if I was going to learn anything to learn it properly. Ten years of music lessons and theory later, I went to law school."

"Do you truly believe that this all will lead to Rutland?"

"Eve there are many things I find truly unbelievable in this world but one thing that I have found to be true on more than one occasion is that with Rutland, the possibilities are certainly endless."

"Top of the morning!" Duncan popped into the kitchen nearly sending us flying out of our chairs followed by Holly.

"Morning Duncan, Holly. Coffee and tea are on the stove. Toast and jam are on the table feel free to enjoy it in the dining room."

Eliza snuck up behind me for a good laugh as she wrapped her arms around me. "You were up early darling, and I can see that you have made quite the start on the first piece to bringing home our Rutland."

"It would seem all those countless hours of learning the great composers has finally paid its dividends. I am not quite sure how it will aid us in our venture but none the less it would be most important that we head back to the church as soon as possible and we will notify Mr. von Winkler with our findings."

"Arthur!" Holly called from the other room. "There is a strange man walking up the driveway."

"It would seem that even he would fit perfectly into this family of unannounced visitors. Be a darling and let him in for me will you." I finished the last bar of music before being bulldozed with his rather charming manner.

"Guten Morgen, Mr. Arthur and I assume you have figured out what exactly we need to do with the, to find you know who…" He looked at me as if he was trying to be discreet in front of the others.

"Hi, how are you sir, no need to be so secretive Arthur has told us all about our next plunder? I am Holly this is my boyfriend Duncan you have already met Arthur and Eliza and this is Eliza's mum Eve."

"Well I'll be, you are as beautiful as Rutland described." Mr. von Winkler grabbed Eve's hand

and greeted her with a kiss. "The name is Chadwick von Winkler and as Arthur may have clued you all in on, is that we are on a mission of sorts to save a man you all thought to be dead. I can assure that Rutland has a reason for everything and as long as we finish this salvage properly, he can explain it to you himself."

"Not for nothing Mr. von Winkler was it? But who are you to Rutland?" Holly demanded answers.

"Fraulein I think these questions might be better answered on the way to the church, yeah!"

We all piled into his quite spacious vehicle and off we went with the newly transposed sheet music in hand.

"Now where was I? Oh yes, you see your uncle and I first met long ago when he took an advertisement out in one of the papers in need of a well-established scientist with backgrounds in quantum electrodynamics, molecular engineering and tad of particle physics. Up until this point everything I had ever worked on in these fields was one theory after another."

"Those are some big fancy words, sir."

"The theories all stopped after Rutland hired me, that man introduced me to the impossible. The ideas most believed to be magic he and I proved with science. I think I have a picture of us in the glove compartment, oh yes here you go." He handed me the picture. "The church was our first headquarters, we opened up shop not too long after Rutland discovered the first of Merlin's doors."

"So you know of Old Merlin?"

"Who do you think helped him duplicate the process of the door? Anyways, we spent months trying to figure out just exactly what it did."

"What did you find in it?"

"We were stepping into uncharted waters for even us, so we brought on board one of the greatest astrophysicist of our time Sir Dieterich Kepler who was a colleague of mine for years in the higher academia."

"And is he still alive?"

"Over the years Rutland and I kept in touch but I am afraid after we parted ways, Kepler was never heard from again."

We arrived to the church with so many more questions to ask but first we need to figure out exactly what the notes hidden in the light sounded like.

"The lights please?" I asked for some assistance as the others looked around the church for anymore of Rutland's possible clues. "Now is this the only piano in this church?"

"It is rumored that Rutland had acquired a piano rarer than the one you are currently sitting at." Von Winkler pitched in.

"But this piano is well worth forty thousand pounds, if it were to go to auction."

"It is a beautiful piano but I am afraid it is not the one we are looking for and will do us no good to play the music you transposed on it."

We sat on the second pew from the front stifled by the very whereabouts of the piano we were in need of. I put the prayer kneeler down and decided to give it a go as it couldn't hurt. My knee hit the cushion and the floor opened up as the pew began to move leading us to a stair case.

"Hold on dear boy." We sat back until the pew had stopped

"The smallest details and the finest touches!" He was always one with a plan even if most of it was inside his head. "Eliza can you grab the flashlight from Rutland's office. It will be most useful for everyone to come into the sanctuary at once."

We counted every step down into an otherwise wide open room with a cruddy old piano in the corner.

"Come here shine the light Arthur. Do you know what that symbol is?"

"No I cannot say I do, it looks like an old rigidly built piano."

"It is the mark of Bartolomeo Cristofori, he not only invented this piano design but this just happens to be the exact piano played by a composer you are quite familiar with, this is said to be Mozart's first piano."

"Just when I thought this was a cruddy beat up old piano." I laid out my sheet music and asked for a light. I began to play a hauntingly gorgeous melody of Amazing Grace. As I continued the solemn rendition, the room began to rotate, walls shifted and a map appeared on the ceiling as lights turned from the floor pointing upward.

"Extraordinary!"

"You have seen this before?"

"Well something quite similar but not this majestic."

"Hold on we need more answers from you before we go any further."

"Fair enough, you see the three of us were partners in this venture of science and making the impossible a reality. We had one hard and fast rule which was, we were never to go meddling in each other's work."

"Then how did any of you get any work done?"

"Let me explain, you see Findas was the first of three worlds that we designed and each of us only upon completion of the three were to look after one. Never were we to ever enter another's world, under any circumstance."

"Wait so you are telling me that you all are responsible for the first light of Findas?" Eve spoke up.

"Yes in the beginning we created Findas,

and then we duplicated the process two more times. Giving birth to two more worlds, Adelmar and Hellondal."

"So I take it that Findas belonged to Rutland?"

"And Adelmar was mine and Hellondal belonged to Kepler. Like I was telling you before, we made a pact that under no circumstance was any of us to enter another's world. The reason for this was so that we could keep balance between the three."

"Since you are here, I am guessing Kepler did not uphold his end of the bargain?"

"More or less, he was in it for his own glory and wanted to be master of all three but since he couldn't technically go into the other worlds, he raised up an army in Hellondal and brought them one by one into this world and then eventually into Findas and now Adelmar."

"So how is that finding Rutland is going to help us?"

"Well after Kepler sent his most feared leader Agnar from Hellondal into Findas, Rutland made sure I closed off the way until it was safe. We met up two weeks ago to devise a similar plan of attack to take back Adelmar from the grasp of the wicked Keres."

"Don't you speak that name, in my, presence!" Eve seemed perturbed by the utterance of Keres. "She is pure evil, born of a darkness not of any world known to man she came to Findas once before and failed but not before taken innocent lives."

"Her power stems from the one who gave her life, through jealousy and rage he called her from the grave and promised her the world."

"You mean that Kepler wanted part in all three worlds."

"Precisely, he slipped portion of dark matter into the process, giving him cloaked access to our worlds. Now with Findas back into order I called upon Rutland to help restore order to Adelmar, only the way in was cut off from the inside and it would seem he may be under Keres' power."

"In light of all of this it was wise for you to find us now we need to figure out just what exactly all of this means." I pointed to the ceiling that currently held a projected image of our current world with no clue as to our next move.

"I may be able to help with that." Eliza stepped forward and pulled from her pocket a cloth bag. "You see, Merlis of the line of Merlin gave this to me with instructions to use it when in need of some enlightening."

"Well go on what is it?"

"I am not quite sure." Eliza reached into the pouch and pulled a handful of sparkling powder out. "Back up, I have no idea what this will do exactly but it's worth a shot."

She tossed it towards the ceiling and to our surprise the powder came to life moving through the light like a free flowing organism with cognitive function, it left an X shaped pattern right in the middle of the Arctic Circle.

"This changes everything." Chadwick gasped. "I have a plane at the airport that can take us here, but you all need to get some more suitable clothes.

"Are we really going to the Arctic Circle? What could possibly be in there?"

"Well if I know Rutland like I think I do and I know him quite well. He hid just as many things as he uncovered, extraordinary things so whatever that X represents I am sure will be of use. Now off we go."

We picked up some cold weather gear to brace for the icy terrain that lay between us and whatever it was we were in need of. The airfield was rather empty nothing but a single cargo plane at the ready.

"We are going to get in that old thing?" Eve asked as the flying machine looked like something out of a junkyard rather than a way of being transported far and wide.

"Most certainly, this will be plenty enough plane to make it there and back."

"And just who is going to fly it?"

"Me of course."

"OH how wonderful, just try to get us there

in one piece."

"And I will of course need a co-pilot if you wish to draw straws make your choice please do so in a bit of a rush. The Bathroom is over there make sure all your gear is on the plane, as wheels are up in ten minutes."

"Arthur, come here!" Holly pulled me aside. "I am all for spur of the moment adventure but this is just insanity we are literally going to put our lives in the hands of a man we barely know."

"Well he did say one of us would be copiloting so?" After saying that sentence aloud I realized how crazy the plan actually was. "Look if this is what we have to do to find Rutland and save Adelmar from future ruin then I am all for it." I reminded her what was at stake. "So the plane is older and the pilot a little more experienced than we would like, but what other option is there."

If I learned anything from Rutland's salvaging journals is that sometimes a strong front can keep the entire team from crumbling even if you yourself are falling apart from the inside. Truth is, I hated all things that dealt with cold climates and or snow of any kind.

"All aboard, please buckle up as we prepare for takeoff." Chadwick began pressing more buttons then I would care to understand. "Did you lot pick straws yet?" He asked as we looked all but at him. "Alright then, Arthur please join me up front as I will need a co-pilot for the takeoff and landing procedure."

"Lovely, first time in a plane and I am asked to co-pilot. We may not make it home after all." I said under my breath.

"I beg your pardon." Chadwick asked.
"Nothing at all. Off we go shall we?"

"That's the spirit, up and away we go!"

The plane raddled the entire length of the runway as the wind whispered over the nose of the plane and around the tale. It took some time but eventually we were able to level off and set course for the Arctic Circle. The site was truly extraordinary as we were thousands of feet in the air without a care in the world.

"Have you ever been to the Arctic?"

"Not in some while I am afraid, it was our first major discovery in one of the ten major ice shelves that bonded us forever. I was cut off from the rest of the group, then out of nowhere your Uncle Rutland came sliding through the ice dropping us into a chamber of sorts. Walls glowing of a reflective liquid that was warm to the touch but never seemed to melt the ice around it."

"The ice broke through?"

"Not exactly, it was more like the ice shifted leading us to discover the very crystal like mineral that we used to power each of our worlds."

The plane began to sway as we made our

final descent. "Everyone please fasten your seatbelt and say a prayer."

The looks on their faces were a mix of petrified and uncertainty. I on the other hand tossed up a prayer of most certain travesty.

"You can land this can't you?"

"O yes I have done it numerous times just not so much in these weather conditions."

The plane rapidly fell towards the horizon that was blended into the frosty air. "On my go pull up on your wheel. Wait for it! Now, Pull!" The wheels touchdown on the icy runway as we skidded along coming to a very lengthy stop. "Is everyone alright?"

"Just peachy!"

I let down the hatch of the main hull to the plane as we were met by a shadowy figure holding a single lantern in one hand and a rope leading back to a path of the runway.

"Come on now, we have no time to get caught out in this wintery hell." The man called out through the snow filled air.

"Russel is that anyway to greet an old friend."

"Chadwick, old is a perfect way to describe yourself, but I would call us friends on a need to go basis. As in once this storm passes you need to go."

"I am afraid that is not possible." I cut in as the door closed behind us. I reached out my hand. “My name is Arthur Sherwood and we are here in hoping to find the next clue leading to the whereabouts of my Uncle Rutland.”

“Rutland you say?” He slid over to the counter. “You missed him by about a week. He was in and out, didn’t go very far.”

“Did he find what he was looking for?”

“I am afraid what he was looking for found him first!”

Chapter 4

The tin shack like building at the edge of the runway was cozy enough for one person to inhabit but not the likes of our crew. There was a map on the wall over the desk that has seen its better days behind it, a cot in the corner that had been well rested in and the toilet was cornered off by some boxes. It smelled of isolation and rum, with a hint of mystery.

"So where exactly will we be staying the night?"

"In here with me of course. I will have the sleds at the ready in the morning but for now I would most certainly enjoy your company as it has been a while since I last had a decent conversation with an actual person."

"Sleds?" I shrugged.

"You heard me correctly, where you will be heading only can be reached by the guidance of my dogs which will pull you along via the sleds."

Eliza chimed in quickly. "I am sorry did I just hear you correctly? We are going to be carted around on dog drawn sleds?"

"Not to worry my dear, Russel has the most elite of pups at his command and never once failed us in the past." Chadwick added for reassurance.

"You have about a four hour sled ride out to the point I lost connection with Rutland. I am not sure what happened exactly but a quick flyby proved to be most useful." He pulled out pictures of Rutland's campsite with coordinates to match.

"And you are positive you did not see him anywhere?"

"Look I have lived in these parts for the better half of my later years in life and I can tell you, from my mouth to God's ears that his dig site was abandoned. It would appear that there was a struggle of sorts but unfortunately no sign of life left to be found."

"Do you know what Rutland was after?"

"Why would Russel have any knowledge of this business of ours?" Chadwick cut in.

"He is the last one to be in contact with Rutland before he disappeared maybe just maybe

Rutland was able to get him a message of sorts? Anyways, what is it to you if I ask him a simple question or two?"

Russel waiting for his turn to speak finally addressed the entire group. "As you all know Rutland played things close to the chest and as it were I have hidden many of items over the years for him as a sort of outside man."

"Oh really you expect us to believe that you worked with Rutland without my knowledge?" Chadwick became snide.

"Who do you think helped him discover and destroy the fountain of youth because as most people believed it to be somewhere tropic he decided to seek it out elsewhere? I just so happened to be the only one in town with the means to get to where he needed to be."

"I read about that discovery in his journal but you were nowhere to be found."

"And rightfully so, because if people could link me to him then surely enough your friend Kepler would have followed suit and I would be a goner for sure. This business isn't for the person who keeps many friends only need to know acquantances."

"So what is it that he had you hide?"

"Like I was saying the fountain of youth was found in the first glacier of the last ice age on his very first trip up this far into the arctic and when we realized its power to corrupt, we destroyed it and scattered the remaining stone throughout the world. I believe he used two of the stone figures as a transport to Findas, but none the less after we cleared out the fountain we created a safe space for all things that need extra watch."

"And just what did he give you to keep watch over?" Eliza wondered.

"An item so powerful that it can both give life and take it away in an instant it's made of minerals and metals not of this world but with the correct tongue it can make an entire world disappear forever. It is the capsule of the Council of the First Light of all the ages. In it holds both time and space for Findas, Adelmar and Hellondal."

"No one was to know about any of it." Chadwick seemed preturbed.

"And yet here you are and here I am knowing all too well everything about it. Look the capsule is a failsafe should anyone of the three lands be overrun by dark matter. So when I knew what he was after I had feared the worst. Which brings me to my next logical question, do you even have a way into Adelmar after you retrieve the capsule?"

"I am afraid we are still working on the logistics as my normal route had been sealed off."

"By Kepler no doubt? I warned Rutland that man was a treasoness venom and not to be trusted." Russel sipped from his tin can.

"It is far worse than simply Kepler I am afraid but one of his associates, she goes by the calling of Keres and is well versed in a magic so dark that there is no return but through death." Chadwick spoke up.

"Like she is a witch?" Eliza hesitantly.

"Oh no don't be silly my dear, she is a sorceress, whose powers are as old as time and as dark as before first light." Chadwick continued on.

"Please do not speak of this treacherous creature any longer." Eve turned away in a moment.

"Mum what are you going on about?" Eliza put her hand on Eve's shoulder. "You know of the one he speaks?"

Eve breathed in the cool arctic air. "Look your father was a good man but even good men can lose their way. Keres preyed upon your father's weakness and allowed Agnar to ascend the throne. She is pure evil in every sense of the word and form. The vanity in it all is that she possesses every desirable trait one would deem irresistible. The only way to truly conquer such corruption is to stay in the light for only there are you safe from her darkness. To walk in any darkness at all is to walk in it completely."

A chilling air moved accrossed the oddly cornered room as if there were no walls at all around us.

"How about some more wood for the fire?" Russel stoked the flame. "What's the story with the silent couple?"

Though Holly and Duncan could keep up a good conversation from ever ending they were to be the ears only as sometimes you need people listening to every detail. "Just shy ofcourse. Maybe a little overwhelmed from the landing." Duncan nodded.

The rest of the night we huddled by the warmth of that fireplace in the middle of the room with a single hole in the roof to let out the smoke. We awoke to the sounds of heavy breathing and barking on the outside of our stay. The fire was still burning with embers as the sun glistened off the frost kissed windows. Russel had wrangled up three sleds and his entire pack of trusty companions ready for the day's journey.

"Arthur and Eliza you will be with Jasper at the front of the pack. Eve and I will be with Rugo and Holly and Duncan you will be led by Ella. Chadwick you will stay here and not break anything."

"Sounds delightful." Chadwick boasted as it was not his style to roll up his sleeves.

"Ladies on the front of your sleds pass the reigns to your driver. Lad's on my ready give the command to your pack leader."

We flew out the gate like a horse down

the track with the snow laden air whipping past our faces leaving the slightest layer of ice on our hoods and scarves. It was an exhilarating feeling riding on the back of the sled as we trekked for miles to Rutland's base camp.

We paused a brief moment as Eliza pulled out her binoculars. "It is just up on the horizon we are approximately four miles out."

"Onward we go and remember to carefully exit your sled when we arrive."

Russel gave the command to pull back on the reigns as the sleds came to a sliding stop. Duncan hopped off his sled first and cleared the area before we took over what was left of Rutland's camp.

"I will get the fire started, we could be in for a long night!"

"Eliza will be with me and Duncan while the rest of you get our accommodations ready. Here take this." I handed Holly my back up firearm that I had tucked away in my boot as this expedition was more about survival than salvaging.

"Just be careful out there exploring and make sure Duncan gets back to me."

"Holly, we will be fine, what could possibly be out there worse than a Drak'on?" I laguhed.

"I don't know? With your luck probably a yeti?"

"Don't be silly Holly, yetis aren't real?"

"That you know of and last time I checked we are currently trying to gain access to another magical land that is currently under the spell of an evil witch. So please be careful!"

"Scouts honor."

We moved quickly through snow covering the last tracks left behind for us by Rutland. Duncan was an excellent tracker even in the most harsh of weather conditions.

"These prints are merely days old and are not the likes of Rutland's."

"What are you saying?"

"The first set belong to someone easily twice his size and the second set belong to that of a woman, it is quite possible however that the indentations aren't that of a larger man but one who was carrying another on their back."

"Duncan! Arthur! Over here quickly."

"What is it?" We ran to her as quickly as one could move through the snow.

"Hand me the shovel from your pack."
The shovel clanked against something rather large hiding beneath the cool flurry covered surface. We wiped off the top of the trunk only to uncover the containers belonging.

"What does it say?" Duncan asked.

"Property of the Kepler Corporation."

"Let me through." I pulled a mini crowbar from my pack and began to pry at the lock as it just wasn't budging. I decided to use a trick

Rutland showed me once as a child. I took the quick freeze from my pack and sprayed it into the locking mechanism and as it expanded I took one good whack at it.

Eliza lifted the lid to find the container loaded with what looked like explosives. "What would one possibly be doing with all of these out here?"

"Let's bring them back to camp and see if Russel can explain their purpose." We left a marker at where we found the crate just in case we needed to find our way back.

"Will you be the one holding them?" They both looked at me like I was short a few apples.

I held the crate in my lap all the way back to the camp where Russel helped me unload.

"Kepler always did like to do things with a bit of a bang. I am afraid however that if he left this behind then it is possible that he found what he needed and we may be at a dead end."

"For Adelmar's sake, I pray you are wrong." We turned in for the night as each of us took watch by the fire, just in case we had any unexpected visitors. The air crystalized as we huddled close together, Eliza took a squeeze to me as I kept a lock onto the rifle Russel supplied the watchers with.

"I wonder what Adelmar is like? I mean like, will it be like Findas?" she asked inquisitively.

"The more I think of it, the more I realize how much Findas was a reflection of who Rutland is. The people are of a diverse nature with a sense of adventure in every fiber of Findas' being. So if I am to guess what Adelmar is to be like?"

"You would say that it is everything Chadwick Von Winkler is?"

"Yes, I imagine it to be filled with all kinds of creatures and people alike. Vibrant with colors and loaded with imagination. You do remember that outfit he was wearing the first time we encountered him."

"Oh don't remind me! It was a horrid hodgepodge of oranges, browns, gold fringe and that hat was just pure silly."

"Yes, exactly and I am sure that Adelmar has all the quarks to match a man of his taste."

"Well it looks like Rutland is going to have to figure this one out on his own." She bellowed. Duncan and Holly woke up to relieve us of our post. As I took one last glimpse at the stars it dawned on me that maybe those sheets of music were hiding more than just some missing notes. I grabbed the handwritten copies I had made before we left to ensure the survival of the originals.

"Arthur what are you doing? I am freezing and tired and just want to get a little shuteye before morning."

"This can't wait as I need the stars to be my

guide." I took the knife from my pocket and began to poke holes where the missing notes were to be on the staff of the music then filled them in on a piece of notebook paper. I repeated the process until I made it through every last piece of music and then held the final product up towards the heavens. "Exceptional!"

"Babe come get some sleep I am freezing in here."

"On my way love." I made sure to freeze frame that sky in my mind for the morning as it will hopefully unlock the path we seek.

The sun came up on the horizon glaring off the icy peaks of the Arctic's rebounding surface. For three hours of sleep I couldn't tell if I was well rested, sleep deprived or just frozen stiff.

"Mmmm that smells delicious." Russel was preparing our breakfast.

"I never make a run into the wilderness without a healthy supply of pork slices, potatoes and sausages. Everyone eat up you will need the calories for today's search."

"You don't have to ask me twice." We ate as well as one can in the conditions we found ourselves in. I spent most of the morning figuring out our best chance at finding a direct route to the coordinates that were left on the notebook paper from the previous night's epiphany.

"So two of us should go north and another group set out east while two remain at camp and we will rotate."

"That will not be necessary as I have narrowed the search area by only a square kilometer; the rest of us will head out while you Russel should man the base camp. If we are not back within the day fear not we have either found our way or are already dead. Either way head back to Mr. von Winkler."

"Simple enough, stay here and in the next solar change you are not back, leave! Good luck and God Speed."

We saddled up our snow shoes as this was not a trek worth putting the pack of dogs at risk for. Before leaving, Russel bestowed upon us water and nourishments for the journey ahead. This would be our most daring adventure yet.

"How far did you say we are from the search area?" Eve asked as she struggled with the snow.

"About ten kilometers north not too far now." It was rather quite far but I find it best to be mind over matter at this point.

"I'm not sure why anyone would hide anything in this disaster of a terrain, like the idea of it is simple put it where no one would dare go but now that you need people to get to it in order to survive most certain death it seems counterproductive." Eve wasnot amused.

"On the bright side mum the faster we find Rutland and set Adelmar free the sooner you get back to Findas which has never seen a single snow flurry a day in its existence."

"And what a glorious reunion that shall be." Eve looked at peace.

"I miss the fresh dirt of the Shadoway beneath my feet as I would go out on the hunt for supper." Duncan reminisced.

"We can always go back my dear." Holly chimed in trying to be supportive.

"Only when the time is right, and Eliza is ready for my throne." Eve concluded.

We trudged onward as we could only bare the frost bitten air a little longer we passed around one of the warm thermos bottles Russel gave to us to keep us warm. "Arthur! What is happening to it?"

The container was glowing brighter with each step until it stabilized to a constant light.

"Quick everyone pull out the other thermoses Russel gave us." Sure enough each had that same glow and to our surprise none of them were filled with water only a wet like substance that seem to heat up with every inch we gained closer to the search area.

"Eliza do you still have that powder Merlis gave you?"

"I do. But how could the powder be of any use to us now?"

"Let me have a look and I will show you." I tossed the powder into the stream of wind that was pushing past us on the eastern side of our current position. It whirled a pathway through the air like a canoe on a river. "And now we follow."

"Rutland has certainly wore off on you."

"I am afraid I cannot take full credit for this as I figured out what that powder from your pouch was last night when I was reading through his Unbelievable Guide to Discovering the Impossible! In simple he and Merlin discovered a magnetic powder that they could alter to be used as a bread crumb of sorts in times of needing to find their way back to a specific secret place that no one else has been to. The reason he hid things so well is that he knew that one would simply not be able to stumble upon these objects by accident."

"So you are saying that the powder is like a living organism with a mind of its own?"

"To an extent yes but again he used it only to react with a specific frequency that way it will only find that which he had kept hidden."

We moved along the gasp of wind until it took a turn straight into the ground. I bent down to find familiar red ribbon pushing through the snow. With a quick pull I was looking at a golden key and arrow that Rutland use to fiddle with all day long in his office. "Rutland was most certainly here!" I pocketed the trinkets.

We started to dig, deeper and deeper into the icy shelf until we struck a metal like object with three cylindrical pathways leading to the center.

"Fantastic another dead end." Eliza seemingly frustrated.

"Not necessarily!" Eve spoke up as she grabbed one of the containers from my pack. "This may not be exactly the same as the one I helped Rutland design in Findas but if I am correct it is a Hallowed Box, this should do the trick."

She poured out each thermos one by one as the object filled to capacity, the ice began shifting around us, and we braced ourselves for whatever was to happen next.

Chapter 5

The ice splintered as it moved beneath our feet, the Hallowed Box submerged deep into the surface as it formed a downward slope. I quickly grabbed the ice pick from my belt as Duncan punctured his dagger into the ice shelf holding onto Holly as I held onto Eliza. Eve was already on her way down.

"You have to let go. Trust me." Her voice faded to the fall.

"Mum!" Eliza shrieked.

"Duncan don't let me go!" Holly terrified.

"Arthur don't you dare drop me!" Eliza squeezed my arm even tighter.

Duncan and I looked at each other, looked down and then back up. "Here goes nothing." We released our grips from the only thing keeping us from entering the great unknown. Which in some way with a brief moment of dawning I realized that all that the unknown was, is simply the undiscovered.

The girls on the other hand screamed the entire way down which isn't a slight to them in the least, we just deal with fears differently as I internalize almost always, they make sure to expound all emotion without consequence.

In a moment our world was to be flipped upside down as the light escaped and birthed us through to the other side of what appeared to be a cavern like inlet sitting slightly below a waterfall. I separated the curtain of water as it fell to the river bed below, the colors burst into the cave blurring our vision until our eyes were able to readjust.

"It's magnificent, truly extraordinary. Do you guys see this?" I asked the rest of the crew to make sure I was all there.

"What is it?"

"Well if I am reading Rutland's guide correctly we are in Adelmar." As I peeked through to other side of the rushing water my fears were made certain.

"Well is there a way out of here or not?" Duncan asked impatiently as he preferred the heights of trees over the uncertainty of streams.

"It would seem that we have entered Adelmar through the Great Fall of the Valley Etern."

"Let me guess the only way out is down?" Eliza and the others came to the same conclusion I had previously thought to myself.

"Unfortunately yes but lucky for us Rutland mapped out the perfect landing spot. We simply need just a little running start and hope we miss the six foot ledge waiting for us at the bottom as anything past that is a good thirty meters in depth."

"You are going off an old drawing of Rutland's on this one are you?"

"It is the best chance we have on account that it also says entry into Adelmar through the Great Fall is a one way ticket as all travelers will need to find another passage to which they came."

"Well isn't that just exciting? If we do ever find Rutland, might we have a little sit down chat with him about his methods of travel?" Holly seeming less than delighted for the plunge.

"Duncan you lead the way and I will follow up as we wouldn't want anyone to stay behind."

Pushing out into the open air as the sun gleamed off the droplets of water now permeated to our clothes we entered into the thunderous roaring river below. One by one we popped up onto the shore with our adrenaline pumping full sigh of relief could be understood amongst the group.

"Never in my life will you ever, I mean ever

get me to do that again." Duncan again reassured us of his terrible relationship with water.

I looked back up at where we had just descended upon realizing now that maybe I should have tried to figure out another way, but I always find it best not to dwell in the past.

"Let's dry off and find a place to set up camp." We waded over to the bank of the river as we scrunched out our clothes and laid what we could to dry on the rocks before us.

Lucky for us our cold weather gear was just enough fabric to build a makeshift shelter as Duncan and Holly worked on building a fire.

We would have to do with what limited meals we had on us, as we were not familiar with the terrain we were in and best not to put anything in your body you are not already acquainted with. I learned that the hard way on my only trip to South America, half of my trek was to whatever I could hide behind enough to relieve my on going upset stomach, on that particular salvage.

"To think that we are a group of people from two separate worlds coming together to save a third world from ruin." Eve pondered a moment.

"A quite interesting one at that, I have never in all my life seen such a beautiful assortment in color of the landscape."

We laid out by the fire with a changing of the guard every two hours to make sure nothing of ill will would come to our camp in this foreign place. I sat up reading everything I could find in this guide on Adelmar. Some of it as usual was just pure Rutland nonsense sandwiched between some very necessary details. His mind always rattled with ideas beyond the right in front of you.

"Exceptional, it says here that Adelmar formed on the last day of darkness like a bunny being pulled from a hat onto the center stage under the blaring spotlight of the sun. That it was a place for all to co-create an existence based on the very foundation of unconditional love in accountability. That their only limitation be found in a lack of imagination. Every life has value and on those days that they show fit to be unworthy to such a civilization such as Adelmar, the people surround the individual and remind them of their value to the very place they find life."

"That is lovely and all but is there anything about Mr. Von Winkler and his part in all of this."

"I am afraid not, only a message to any visitors of the land. 'If you wish to survive the vastness of this place, you must first unlock the magic inside of your own soul.'"

I sat up pondering the very idea of magic as in our world it was simple sleight of hand or an idea so well-conceived that it can alter ones perception to actual reality. The further I was able to get my logical thinking past simple ideas I found my thoughts wandering to the impossible.

"You alright Arthur?" Eve came over to stay watch with me as she sent Eliza off to bed.

"I am, so to speak, I just can't understand for the life of me why anyone would want to destroy such beautiful places as Findas an Adelmar."

"Power my dear is a constant temptation for most and when it goes unchecked it turns into a pride that cannot be reasoned with, and once you have it they will do anything to keep it."

"This photo of the three of them, would make one believe that they were inseparable."

"In the beginning it would seem that all things were as they were meant to be. In Findas it is said that the Keeper of Keepers decided it best that no magic at all be used with in the land as he didn't want even the slightest chance for the dark magic that ravished the first world the three of them created to find its way in."

"The first world?"

"Calestar was a group effort and is only briefly mentioned in the ancient writings of my world. It was destroyed and in promising to never destroy another creation the Keeper of Keepers set forth a decree that under no circumstance should another creator enter a world that was not their own. He had Merlin cast a spell over the entryways of Findas so that nothing of any sort of magic could enter."

"So that is why Kepler sent Agnar to Findas as he knew Merlin's Doors would keep Keres out."

"Precisely you see for Kepler was never on the same level as Chadwick and Rutland. He allowed his envy to turn into jealousy until finally he decided that he wanted them all. Some even believe that an outsider was the true cause of the First War of Findas. From what we now know it would seem that outsider is none other than Kepler."

"So he just wanted to conquer the other worlds and be able to roam freely through out them."

"If only it were that simple, I fear he was trying to merge the three worlds enslaving the inhabitants of both Findas and Adelmar."

"Yeah but only this time it won't be against mere men or women but principalities not of any world. I have heard stories of a dark magic that ravished Calestar leaving only but one surviving elder and their family."

"Duncan, you know of Calestar? But how, those stories are only found in the royal writings of Findas." Eve pondered.

"I may have been born in the Shadoway but my great grandfather was given a safe haven in Findas right at first light. My lineage comes from Calestarian descent and my father made sure I never forgot where we came from but to also not let anyone know until it was of use."

"Well I guess now is a good of time as ever." I headed off to bed as they stood watch for the remainder of the night. The stars were as innumerable as my world only more vibrant in color, I started to count as I nodded off to sleep.
"Arthur!" Eliza began to shake me. "Wake up! Come take a look at this."

I moved at my usual morning pace and put on my glasses as I sat up with in the make shift shelter we formed from the nearby shrubbery. "I'm up, I'm up!"

She led me up a path and onto a look out point. "It is just over there beyond rivers end."

We were looking upon what seemed to be a village of sorts but uncertain of which side of the current situation the residence of such a place stood we had to do our recognizance work swiftly as one wrong move in a place like this, meant imminent death. And with a swooping sound a hawk like bird grazed past our heads letting out a screeching call.

"Get down, we need to make our way back to the others." We moved with quick pace as we feared that our presence in this land was surely noticed.

"Everything alright? What's the hurry?"

Duncan asked.

"Pack what you need, we must move at once."

"Where exactly are we moving to? We have not the slightest idea of this place and you just want to up and move."

"Look, we saw a village of sorts by the rivers end and we are not sure if we may have tripped one of their alarms, look…" It was then I noticed the Sherwood family crest with an arrow and key, branded into the tree next to a narrow path. "This way, with a little pep please."

"Are you sure this is the correct path?"

"Yes it is, I am most certain." I said with a smile as I touched the crest carved into the tree before squeezing onto the path that led us to another crest. "You see Rutland always had a thing for narrow paths and leaving his mark everywhere he went. Knowing that he would need to possibly find his way back or even be found himself, it would seem he left a breadcrumb trail that anyone who knew him would recognize."

"He always said. 'When in a place unknown it is best to take the road less traveled.'" Eve did her most splendid of Rutland impressions. "As it is often the wiser option when needing to go undetected."

We walked with precision as we neared the end of the brush. Snapping upward a trap had sprung from beneath our feet leaving us suspended into sky of the very top branch of the tallest tree one could see. A figure moved below us as he started to lower the contraption. Our hearts raced at the same rate as more figures moved in below us.

"And that is why you must always be prepared for anything." The man lectured the others waiting for us. "Now what business do you have in this part of Adelmar? Or any part of Adelmar for that matter and why should we not simply kill you and move on with our day?"

"Rutland?" I saw him before he could see us as the trap only had but a few holes for its capture to breathe out of.

"Arthur? Is that you my dear boy?"

"Yes now cut us down immediately!"

"Us? Who is with you?" He inquisitively asked bringing us down the trap unfolded.

"Just the usual crew plus..." His face turned red at the sight of her majesty.

"Eve I am…" She slapped the words right out of his mouth as he turned to the rest of the group. "I may have deserved that just a tiny bit."

"How dare you leave us thinking you were dead?" She was angry but joyous in her approach. "Not even a letter or anything?"

"I left Arthur the bottle of ink." Rutland responded knowing that she meant from him to her.

"Sometimes you are the most infuriating

person I've ever known."

"And other times?" He pulled her close as her eyes welled up with tears.

"Charming and irresistible, but don't you think for one second that those qualities will let you off the hook. Care to explain all of this?" She waived her arm through air as if to signal everything around them.

"Yes, of course, right you are in need of an explanation but maybe first we bring you into the village."

"Excuse me Mister Rutland." A young man approached us with quite the heavy Bengali accent. "Will these guests be joining us for tonight's festivities?"

"Sensational idea Dipaka, go at once and make sure they have a place at the table. Please make sure Girish is alerted of our company." Rutland agreed.

He was off in a hurry as the rest of the group carried up the rear. We made our way to the village at the foot of the mountain. The colors as expected were a vibrant kaleidoscope of wonder, music carrying on throughout the village as shades of red orange purple and green clouds were being tossed into the air by villagers passing on by.

"I don't mean to make a big deal of this but your friend Mr. von Winkler seems to think that Adelmar is facing Armageddon and here you are just living it up among the people like you're on holiday?"

"Oh relax Arthur we currently are observing one of Adelmar's most long standing rituals. The Noterian as it were is a week free of magic where the people live as they once did in peace with in the natural law of the land. Also, how is old Chadwick?"

"He is fine, no kookier than I would assume him to be. But what of this Keres?"

"Keres is powerless during this time. No need to worry we can talk of that come morning there is plenty of time until the uprising." He turned and pushed the large door open that led to the center of the festival. I felt like I was back at a bazaar on my travels to India. We were greeted with flowered neck garb and a thick colorful juice like beverage.

"These are gorgeous, did you make these?" Eliza asked the group of girls who simply giggled at us before running on their way.

I took the first sip, over taken by the array of fruity flavors, I paused. "Delightful what is in it?"

"That is a Noti secret I am afraid. Please make sure you save some for the toast." We looked up to see Dipaka waiting for us. "Welcome to the village of Noti. Let us take your belongings to your huts." He bowed as a few men came along side us and relieved us of our luggage which wasn't but a few bundled up sacks that seemed useful at the time of departure.

"Are you guys seeing what I am seeing?" Duncan pointed out the biggest supper table any eye has ever feasted upon in our lives.

"Ah yes on each night during the Noterian, the entire village sits down for one big feast as they remember the world they once loved." Dipaka continued as these large elephant like creatures made their pass by the tables delivering the food prepared for tonight's menu. "Don't mind the Canantars, they are gentle creatures at heart."

We passed serpent charmers, jugglers, mind readers, flame breathers, jewelry makers all leading up to the grand entry of Girish. He was dressed from head to toe in brightly colored silk and he wore a hat befitting of such an occasion. "My people! On the fifth night of the Noterian we bring thanks for the troubled times as it is in these moments we grow stronger as a nation. Now let us partake in the first drink. Here! Here!"

We raised our glasses in cheers. The drums played with a mighty roar as the night's entertainment moved into the form of dancing.

"Forgive me Dipaka but what does the rest of Adelmar do during the Noterian?" I asked curiously.

"This is all of what is left of Adelmar. Unfortunately the other nations have come under the control of Keres."

"Like mind control?" Eve inquired.

"For those who submit to Keres' will, were spared but the rest who fought back were led to the slaughter. The Noti people, our people were marked from birth that no dark magic may corrupt their souls."

"But enough talk of the dark times." Rutland sat down beside us. "How is the salvaging business holding up?"

"Well it has been a slower process than I would have liked but nothing short of unbelievable."

"I see you have learned a thing or two from my journals."

"Oh yes once I got passed all the nonsense." I pulled his 'Unbelievable Guide to Salvaging the Impossible' out of my pocket and opened it to some of his doodles. "What on earth were you on when you did these?"

"So you know how I told you once that when surviving in any terrain it is important to know your types of vegetation?"

"Yes I vaguely remember that conversation."

"Well this happened before that." We both had a good laugh. "I was lost in the hills of Halle as it were during my first exploration into Findas. I was trapped by some falling rock. With just the water on me and what I thought were simple berries sent me on the longest ride down loopy lane I have ever been on?" He seemed confused.

"Your Uncle danced with the Devil's Lock that day, by the time we found him he had almost gone fully catatonic." Eve joined in.

"I am sorry to be nosy as well but Uncle Rutland if you and your partners created these lands, then how would you not know the difference between Devil's Lock and normal berries." Holly made a logical point.

"With what happened to Calestar." Duncan perched up at the mention of his origins. "We had to put in some precautions with the rest of the worlds. In doing so von Winkler and I shut off the way to all three worlds leaving Kepler trapped in Hellondal."

"What exactly did you do?"

"With the help of Merlin he brewed us a memory elixir laced with breadcrumbs of sorts."

"Meaning that you had no recollection of what you did?"

"In that moment yes but he left just enough clues for us to find our way back if we ever needed to."

"And what happened to Calestar?"

Rutland seemed dejected. "Kepler overtook its people and its land merging it with Hellondal leaving no survivors but the ones he enslaved. I was only able to find one family refuge in Findas but I am afraid they perished when

Agnar invaded."

Duncan stood up pulling up his sleeve revealing the mark of his people. "What if I told you that before my mother perished she hid me deep in the Shadoway forest only for me to be discovered by one of the First Keepers of Findas?"

"I would say that your parents were the bravest people I ever knew. I would say that if they were here to see you today that they would be more proud of you than any other achievement in their lives."

A certain sadness wept over Duncan as he turned away from the rest of the group. "So if Kepler is stuck in Hellondal he is responsible for both Agnar and Keres, how is it that they have made it into the other worlds?"

"I fear that he may have back doored Merlin's spell leaving open ways hidden throughout the three worlds." Rutland spoke up. "In order to stop him we must first stop Keres, and the odds in this event are not in our favor."

"We defeated Agnar against all possibilities. What is one more?" I spoke confidently.

"You do not understand, she is not flesh and blood, a sword will not simply do. She moves like smoke and can take over that which pleases her in an instance. She was birthed from Kepler's darkness and I am afraid this battle might prove fatal to us all." Rutland spoke as if he had first-hand experience with such darkness.

Dipaka's fear turned into hope as he chimed into the conversation. "There is one person we have yet to seek, but I am most uncertain of his whereabouts and his legend is even bigger than yours Mr. Rutland. No one has ever laid eyes on him and he has never laid eyes on anyone."

"Does he have a name?"

"Most who speak of him, call him Bhoot but that's only because it is said that those who knew him perished many years ago, it is said that all of Adelmar's time both past and present lye with in him. Before Keres entered Adelmar it is believed that he dwelled in a hidden temple somewhere along the Lamba Mountains."

"Can you lead us there?" Rutland asked as we all sat back uncertain.

"I can show you the way but we will not be under the protection of the Noterian as the way which we must seek can only be found by the ancient maps of Adelmar."

"We will leave the day after next and set out with those only needed for this expedition. The rest will stay behind and watch guard as it is more than likely Keres is aware of the unbalance of Adelmar since we have entered this land."

"The Lamba Mountains are not to be tampered with or is the trek for the faint of heart as they are considered holy ground and we must not disturb that which is at rest in such a place."

Rutland, Duncan, Eliza, Dipaka and myself prepared for the journey ahead of us. Holly and Eve stayed behind to prepare the Noti for the days to come.

Chapter 6

The sun peaked through the trees as it was our day to rise up and seize the moment. Dipaka brought us before Girish who would lead us into a small room where the ancient maps of Adelmar had been sealed. “It is with great honor that I bestow this quest upon a crew worthy of a king’s ransom. For the road may narrow and the path be uncertain, do not lose heart for with you I send the greatest tracker in all of Adelmar. He is the bravest of my men and will lead you to the Lamba Mountains to find Bhoot. I present to you…” Before he could finish the long introduction a man standing no taller than three feet or that of the height of an adolescent child entered the room.

"I am Sankar!" his voice rang out.

Rutland gave him a look of welcome. "No doubt we will be in need of a little luck on this journey, especially now that the Noterian is coming to a close."

"I will lead you to the one you seek, a place only a few have ever stepped foot and keep us hidden along the way." He pounded his chest before giving out a war like cry.

"Sankar come here at once." Girish pulled him in as he whispered to him, Sankar nodded.

"Forgive me my king." He bowed to Girish in a sign of understanding before turning back to us. "So it is Bhoot, who you seek? I saw him once but it was only in a dream and even then I only caught a glimpse of the back of his head before waking up."

"Is that so? From what we have been told he is as old as Adelmar."

"Yes and No, Mister?" He looked at me.

"Arthur, Arthur Sherwood this is Eliza, Holly, Eve and Duncan. You already know Rutland."

"It is true that he is old but not quite as old as Adelmar, for the story goes. When he was a boy he helped his father heard their sheep along the Lamba Mountains. One day one of the sheep strayed from the pack and so as his father taught him, he corralled the rest of the heard in early to go look for the sheep but it is said he never returned. That day his father told of his bravery and that some days he could feel him in the wind. It is believed that Bhoot stumbled upon the first holy temple of Adelmar and released the magic throughout the land becoming the source of all its powers he has remained hidden from the people. But that was hundreds of years ago."

"And you believe he is alive?"

"It is in the ancient writings that one day when he dies the magic will die with him. That he allows the ability to tap into the magic as a sign that he is with us." Girish concluded as he tossed the map into the air, it came alive before our very eyes.

"We will trek around the first of the three mountains and come up the back side of the Lamba range. We must layer up as where we are going there is no room for error. One mishap and we all turn into ice."

It seemed silly at the time that we would need to layer up as we were in a rather tropical climate but the map had the Lamba mountain range just shy of the height of Everest with the cave temple of Bhoot two thirds of the way up.

"We must leave at once as Keres will certainly find the rest of the inhabitance of Adelmar by week's end, which gives us three days to journey up to Bhoot." Sankar was most confident in his ability to get us there on time but I was still uncertain as to what good it will do.

A large commotion erupted past Girish's tent as we followed outside to see some of the villagers standing over a man who had seen better days mumbling and bumbling around. An odd looking fellow he was bruised and worn down. Girish and Rutland pushed the group apart to get a better look.

"Chadwick, old boy you look like rubbish." Rutland gasped.

"I am sorry Rutland but did you just call him Chadwick."

"Why yes I did, he like I, is both a salvager and a creator! Adelmar was his, as Findas was mine."

"That's all well and good but I am afraid that someone has assumed his identity because…"

The man rather frazzled sat up with his hand pointing towards the air. "Kepler!" He yelled.

"Oh this isn't good."

"Arthur, what did you do?" Rutland exclaimed.

"Well you see a man claiming to be Chadwick von Winkler brought to us a proposition to help find you, paid us handsomely and all."

"Did you lead him to the access way to Adelmar?" Rutland visually angry.

"Ummm…" I began to stutter.

"Well boy what is it?"

"No, we most certainly did not. We left him

in the arctic circle at the runway tower."

"It is ok Rutland, I shut the way from which I came only after Kepler and I had the scuffle."

"Was it really necessary to fight him?"

"He was wearing my favorite suit!" The man continued on.

"I am sorry but how did you even end up here?" I cut in.

"That arrogant fool had me in the trunk of my own car. Last thing I remember, I was brewing a concoction of sorts in my laboratory and then out cold. When I came to, you were just loading up the cargo plane at the airport. I slipped on board with no one the wiser."

"Still doesn't quite answer how you ended up here?"

"I tracked him down to your campsite and then ambushed him before he could enter the hidden passage. If you are wondering about all of this. Well I always keep a make shift stun-stick on me at all times. Only this time I wasn't as far away as I would have liked to have been. I got blasted here as I can only assume he got knocked out there."

"It was only a matter of time that he would come after Adelmar." Rutland chimed in as Sankar waited patiently hand raised. "What is it Sankar?"

"This is all well and good sir but we must go now for the journey is as I told you. There will be plenty of time to talk along the way."

"Where are you going?" The real Chadwick von Winkler asked.

"The Hidden Temple inside the Lamba Mountains to find Bhoot."

"Oh so you are just going to climb the most dangerous mountain ever created in search of a ghost?"

"What do you know of this?"

"I would know, I…"

"That's enough!" Rutland cut in giving his old buddy Chadwick a very familiar look as he leaned into him. "You know you cannot simply reveal your identity to these people, your people!"

"Right you are as always." He whispered to Rutland. "Have you room for one more on this bold journey?"

"I don't see why not as long as you can carry your own weight." Sankar put out his hand before spitting in it. Chadwick did the same and off we went in search of Bhoot.

We set out to the base of the Lamba Mountains with Sankar at the lead, we followed behind expediently as Dipaka brought up the rear. The terrain was like that of a tropical island, hot and dense with a constant mist in the air. The birds flying overhead were exploding with colors as they made their way through the trees. The insects were bigger than I would have liked. I swatted at the mosquito like creature buzzing around my head.

"Is everything in this world have to be bigger than normal?" After uttering those words I realized that this was normal to this world.

"A few tips for surviving the next couple of days. Stay away from the serpents with black bellies and yellow diamond shaped scales. The white scorpions as well as the moonbas plants."

"Moonbas plants?"

"They appear to be pleasing to the eye but I can tell you that looks are deceiving as one touch will leave the curious party in a state of temporary paralyses."

"And it looks like?"

"That's the thing, it comes in many appearances but the one trait they all have in common is that of the yellow stem. You know now that I think of it, just about anything we stumble upon in Adelmar has a good chance of certain death best to just let instinct guide you."

"Great yes we are wondering in a gigantic death trap. Lovely!" I let out sarcastically.

"Adelmar wasn't always filled with such danger around every corner. It was quite the opposite. The magic was pure and the creatures even more so. I am afraid it be but one dark soul that changed it forever. Contaminated the very make up off this world."

"This is all because of Keres?"

"No, Keres is simply a messenger of the one who may never enter this world. A man so evil that he blends in to the simplest of people like a wolf in sheep's clothes he has led many to slaughter with no one the wiser."

Rutland cut in. "You won't have to worry about him for long. Once we find Bhoot he will set us on the right course to breaking the darkness Keres has poisoned the land with and give it back to the people."

"Whatever land there may be left to give." Dipaka added.

"This land will once again flow purely from the heavens height to the valleys deep, no more darkness or pain or suffering. For the goodness that once was never left but must be simply reminded of the good it held once again." Sankar assured with hope.

"That is quite the profound statement. You would surely make for a fearsome salvager." Rutland patted him on the head. "For at our core, we truly believe that no thing or no one is too far gone."

The jungle air grew denser the further we trekked. Trees hung lower the closer we got to the base of the mountain. A fog like mist formed around us as a breeze flowed off the leaves, we paused to wipe the sweat from our brows as Sankar looked around for a path.

"Three paths to choose from but only one

will lead to Bhoot." Sankar said quivering.

"And the others lead to?" I wondered aloud.

"Death, Mr. Arthur! So let's not pick the wrong one shall we." Sankar gave me a look that I have only given other people but never fully received myself. "Now will you help me clear the way?"

We hacked at the brush until our machetes struck stone. "Halt!"

"Oh come on just push through. Up we go!"

"Are you sure? I mean are you one hundred percent positive? Rutland now is not the time for guesses."

"Look at the other two paths and tell me what you see!"

I paused. "All of the trees and ground push inward with no sign of return."

"Precisely leaving us with option number three, the path no one has travelled." We climbed up and over the wall to the start of a long journey.

"Watch your step and follow my lead." Sankar calmly made his way up the stone staircase marked with symbols of an ancient language.

"Sankar! What is that noise?" Eliza and Holly perked up.

"Nothing to worry about keep up the pace."

Half way up our climb and the loud rumble began getting closer and Rutland along with

Dipaka started sprinting behind us. "We need to move now! The staircase is um well just run!" I looked back for a brief moment to see the trail crumbling behind us, it seemed as though we would never reach the top. Sankar, Dipaka and Rutland made it up to the ledge as Eliza followed with just Duncan, Chadwick and myself bringing up the rear. "Arthur! Grab my hand." Duncan and I jumped as the last stairs fell out, we made it out with not so much as a scratch and an extremely high heartrate.

"You mind explaining just what that was?" Rutland called out Sankar.

"That was someone clearly not following my lead. Now I believe this is the perfect place to get some shut eye for the night. We all need to rest up before we continue."

"And just what are we continuing on into." Rutland demanded.

Sankar looked on into the night. "Seven tests must be complete in order for us to even be worthy of Bhoot's presence."

"Was that one of them?"

"That was simply a welcome to what lies ahead."

Eliza and I began a fire as Sankar took Rutland with him to do some research for our next move.

"Wouldn't be an adventure with Rutland without some sort of challenge." Chadwick scoffed.

"Chadwick I almost forgot you were with us." I honestly did forget he was with us but the truth is whatever was in store for us. We really could use the experience. The fire crawled into the night as we awaited Rutland and Sankar's return.

"The good news is we only have to look ahead of us as it would be impossible for anyone to come up from behind us. The only way out was up. We will move out at first light." Rutland sat next to me as Sankar gave us a rousing speech.

"The seven obstacles will test us in every aspect of our beings. It is said in the ancient writings that Bhoot himself endured seven nights of trial before ascending to his final place on the mountain." He put his head down on the nearest rock he could find as did we all.

I looked into the night sky in wait of what could be anything at all but really that is all fear is anyways. Fear is simply our mind strewing about unseen possibilities rather than to focus on what is in our current control. That is why we must surrender our wills to the better.

Chapter 7

"We must move quickly under the shadow cast by the first light of uprising." Dipaka said in a hush tone as we packed up in a hurry. "Keres has begun to move from the northern region."

"Um, and you know this how?" I pondered.

"Dipaka is a vision caster. His gift is seeing across a distance using his mind as a sort of third eye." Sankar leaned in.

"And on a clear enough day I can see into that which is to come."

"If Dipaka is a Vision whatever, then what is your gift exactly Sankar?"

"I am from an ancient line of Light Shifters." He revealed a ring of a pure diamond like structure.

It sounded quite impressive but we all looked on in bewilderment. Then he took light into the ring and used it to lift a tree out from its roots. "More or less I can use whatever light given to bend matter at will."

"Extraordinary!" I let out. "So if you can use your powers now that means… Oh yes let us get a move on!"

The journey to the first of the seven tests we were to endure, was more pleasant than I had anticipated. Yes we moved rather quickly, but I could never imagine the vast challenge we were to endure. We came to a carved out rock wall with divots spread out just far enough for you to fit a rod in but increments that one would have to make it to the top in order to complete the ladder.

"It is rumored that Bhoot himself climbed this wall without any divots in it and so he challenges those who seek him to a similar challenge under one rule that no magic be used to gain access to him."

"One problem I only see a single rod at the bottom and twelve carved out rows above it." I explained.

"That's why it is called a challenge." Rutland jumped up to grab the rod.

We tried for a good while as each of us

only had the strength to make it up to the seventh row. We took a break to rethink our strategy as I tossed a rock in the air, Rutland paced as Chadwick chimed in most wittingly. "What if we only had to make it up to the fourth row?" He hypothesized.

"Go on Chadwick!"

"What if we carved more rods out of the fallen brush over there and turned it into an actual ladder."

With that in mind we grabbed the rod for measurement purposes and began to carve our way through the first challenge. Dipaka lead the way this time swinging his hips up as he made it to the fourth rung he filled in the first four steps of the ladder. "Alright toss me up another one!" He began to fill in the rest of the spaces. One by one we each made it to the top as I had the pleasure of carrying Sankar on my back which made for a few laughs.

"You know I could get use to this, just need a nectarsmash and some quambee juice and this is the life." Sankar laughed.

"Don't get too comfortable, I couldn't possibly carry you the entire way."

After dusting ourselves off, we walked directly into our next test. Above the opening of the cave read an old forgotten language of Noti, "L' oubeg Am Ambo No'Fi Ve"

"What does it mean?"

"You are in luck." Sankar said.

"Really?" I puzzled.

"You are in luck because as a Light Shifter I am well versed in all languages of this world."

"Well what does it mean?"

"Darkness cast out in secret." He pointed to the way in. "It is believed that in order to be in Bhoot's presence you must first purge yourself of any darkness that may linger, but beware of the way we enter as it will take you to places you never wish to find in your own heart."

The whispers of a past better kept secret emerged from the walls of the cave and all of a sudden I found myself cut off from the group. "Arrrthur!" I heard my sister's voice for the first time in ages. We were at the old swimming hole on the backside of Rutland's property when I looked away for a split second and the rope swing broke. I tried to jump in and save her but the current pulled her straight under. "It is all your fault!" echoed louder and louder but this time it was my parent's voices. I pushed on deeper into the cave.

Led on by the noise of every childhood bully I had ever made an acquaintance with. Sweat dripping down my face with no end in sight I finally collapsed from the exhaustion. A boisterous snapping sound came from above with a little light in the form of a small man echoing behind it.

"Bhoot?" I reached towards the figure shrouded in light.

"What are you doing Arthur? Did you lose your marbles in there?"

"Rutland! How long was I out for?"

"I'd say roughly an hour or sooooooo." Rutland moved further away until he was gone and I was left knowing that I wasn't quite out of the next challenge.

"Oh bullocks." I had to harness my energy into finding a way out of this mess. My breath grew deeper as the darkness closed in on my mind. "Jump!" the voices echoed off the walls in a haunting whisper. "Jump!"

I gave it my best effort and as I landed, the ground beneath my feet gave way to a free fall that flushed out all of my deepest regrets. Tumbling onward and almost out of the rush of light that flooded in from the outer portion of the space I currently occupied a hand reached forward and grabbed me right before tipping over the edge.

"You saved my life!" I gasped as I looked down below only to see the path we started from. "How's it that we fell downwards but are further up the mountain?" I looked to the side as everyone was hanging onto the thin ledge with brief footing.

"We must keep on until we make to the next summit!" Dipaka ordered as we shuffled slowly to the other side.

"Eliza are you okay love?" She turned away.

"She was the first one out followed by Sankar."

"And where is Sankar?" I asked unwillingly.

"He went over the edge." She pushed away. Rutland didn't say a word as he sat seemingly disturbed against the rock. Chadwick and Duncan began to set up a fire for the night as one of the three great lights filled the evening sky.

"Sankar may have left us for a moment but one day we will be reunited beyond the stars as we believe that a life well lived only continues to a place it was designed for."

"Here! Here!" We raised our make shift water pouches and took a sip to remember a man small in stature but mighty in heart.

Sitting around the fire telling stories of journey's past I noticed that Rutland still couldn't seem to shake whatever went on with him in that awful place.

"You alright there Rutland?" I pulled up a patch of dirt right next to him as we looked across the star scattered sky.

"Right now I wish I had a nice bottle of old man Waverley's."

"That bad yeah."

"Arthur when you lived a life as long as I have and never need mind you come across some of the darker parts of humanity that no one should ever be capable of. It wears not only on your mind but your soul." His never ending cycle of life finally caught up to him.

"You have done some things you might have wished were handled in other ways?"

"No regrets what so ever I would live every moment the same all over again." He looked further into the night. "There is one secret I am afraid I can no longer keep."

"Go on you can tell me anything." I pulled out a small bottle of Waverly from my pocket as the key and arrow fell out.

"You read the last page of my guide I see. And what it is you got there?" He looked fondly at the arrow and key.

"Always was one for detail, read it cover to to right where you stopped, twice. I found your old arrow and key set at the pass and figured it might be to something extraordinary so why not bring it along." Hoping he would tell me a grand story to their belonging.

Rutland took a swig. "Nothing of this life or time anyway. Some things are just keepssakes." He Paused. "Well you see Arthur about thirty years ago I had met a woman who I fancied very much. Those belonged to her."

"You talking about Eve?"

"No this is before Findas was ever cast into the stars. She was from Calestar and it was a fast and fiery love. We were inseparable a little over nine months after we met she gave birth to two beautiful children."

"Hold on, you have children? And I never met them and what happen to this beautiful woman?"

"She is somewhere living her life with no recollection of me or our beautiful children."

"And your children?"

"I was able to get them back home but for their safety I left them in the care of a good family."

"Have you seen them since? How old were they?"

"My daughter passed away when she was seven and my son grew up to be a fine young man worthy of the name Sherwood."

"But Cassidy passed away when we were seven. What are you saying Rutland?"

"I was going to tell you when the time was right but I feared that if Kepler knew I had a family of my own that he would surely come after you. So I made sure to be in your life as much as possible without the inkling of who you are." He held up the trinkets. "She was the key to my heart and you two were the arrow that gave my life direction and purpose."

Eliza approached as my mouth was gaped wide staring into the abyss of my entire existence.

"What has him in a toosie?" She asked.

"I think it was that cave that has him still worked up." Rutland answered for me. "Best to give him some space."

"Yeah that cave was absolutely dreadful if you ask me." She moved back towards the fire.

"So Pip and Brunley are not my parents? But how did you convince them to look after me and not to have children of their own?" I was having trouble wrapping my head around the current predicament Rutland had placed before me. Deep down I knew that I was tied to Rutland far more closely than a nephew he put in charge of his estate.

"Fate as it were to be, they simply couldn't have children of their own. So, when I had told them my predicament, they stepped up big time without ever saying a word to anyone. When Cassidy died, I never thought..." Rutland holding back tears. "I am just glad you know now that what I did was always with your best interest in mind, you have become a fine young man."

"But what about Brunley and Pip?"

"They are your parents as much as I am your biological father." It really was a lot to take in, I mean my entire life seemed out of place and for a moment it all started to make sense. "Look Arthur, I have always loved you like a son."

"That's because I am your son! You nit." I spoke quite loosely with him as all the times I ever gave my parents trouble and to find out that they willingly and lovingly took our care on at huge expense to them without hesitation.

"I know but no one else knows that."

"I did actually." Holly piped in. "Don't look so surprised. Everyone in the family knew. You pretend like I cannot keep a secret."

"You didn't think, hey, maybe it's time to tell him the truth?" I looked now at both of them.

"It wasn't mine to tell." Holly backed out.

"Sometimes the truth is best kept for a proper occasion." He rebutted.

"I've been my own man for the better half of a decade, at any time would have been good."

"I chose now and I understand if you only see me doing this as a way to Bhoot and saving Adelmar but I couldn't keep it any longer and by this point I fear Kepler knows of whom you are. I'm sure you have a lifetime of questions? And when we make it out of here I will answer them all."

"Well lets deal with Keres first and we will get to Kepler later. My questions can wait." I said only to give the shocking news a little time to wear off.

Dipaka came over to let us know we had to move on as the next portion of our journey and that it would be safer with a little darkness above our heads.

"You know I could go for a perfect spot of

tea and some of those muffins you made us on Christmas." I looked at my bride.

Eliza laughed. "They are just blueberry muffins with some crushed walnuts and cinnamon on top."

"What is Christmas?" Dipaka asked.

"It's only the most magical time of year." In the moment I now understand I should have used a better word than magical to describe it, but in a world without magic, Christmas is like seeing a rabbit being pulled from a hat for the first time. "So basically it is a time of year where the entire family gets together in one big celebration where people exchange gifts, eat delicious food and drink and be merry."

"So sad that it only happens once a year, we make it a point to do it every week in our culture. Family is important and to celebrate the ones we love is to bring joy to those we care for deeply."

"Well we have other holidays too in which we get together and such. But I see your point."

We trekked on for what seemed like an eternity as we faced our next four obstacles. First we ran through a field of hot ember patches. Second, we bobbed and weaved in formation through a thicket of thorns and moombas plants. Third, we swung across a bottomless pit using but a single vine that led nowhere but up and finally we stand directly in front of a creature so revolting that it made taming a Drak'on look easy.

"I knew this was a mistake and why no one ever returned from seeking out Bhoot."
The creature snarled at us as it moved up to its hind legs, well from my count it had three sets of legs with one set appearing to be arm like with three finger like extensions on the end. A face to remain only in nightmares and about as big as anything we have ever come across.

"Don't move, the Galagus works off its preys fear and moves in only when it senses it can strike." Dipaka then continued to move us all into place as he read the final instruction from the previous challenge. "Those who are worthy of Bhoot may only enter his temple if they can spare the life of one trying to take theirs."

"Oh lovely we have to take this thing on without killing it."

"Don't move Mr. Chadwick, I have placed you out of the path of its sight. We must capture the beast and set it free."

"All suggestions are welcome!" I nodded.
Rutland looked at Chadwick. "Old boy you remember the time in the uncharted islands of the Tazboti."

"Tazboti?" Chadwick looked as if he was racing through his memories. "Oh yes! Yes I do, but do you think it will work?"

"What's the worst that could happen?"

"Usually when you say things like that Rutland we have a ninety-nine percent chance of death!" I chimed in.

"That is why we live our lives in the one percent Arthur!"

Rutland jumped out in front to the Galagus' attention and my, did he ever do it in spectacular fashion. The beastie was all kinds of riled up. The rest of the group passed to the other side unnoticed. "On my go Chadwick throw it."

Rutland shifted his stance. "And Go!" Chadwick tossed a black sphere from his pocket towards the creature as Rutland made his run for it he sliced at the sphere with his favorite knife opening up a sophisticated net like contraption pinning down the Galagus granting us safe passage to our next and hopefully final challenge.

"What the heck was that?" Duncan seemed mesmerized by it.

"A little invention I perfected after Rutland and I ran into some trouble back in Tazboti. You think monsters are only from other worlds?"

"Can I have one?"

"Of my netters? Sure you can!" Chadwick placed it in Duncan's hand. "It is only for temporary capture of anything you wish no harm as the net dissolves."

We entered into the temple of Bhoot, the door swung wide open and the silhouette of a man in meditation appeared before our very eyes. Dipaka took a knee in reverence as we all followed suit.

"Hoooooowummmmm!" A deep voice echoed. "Why have you come to seek me only now?"

"Your Holiness if I may, Adelmar is at risk of total annihilation at the hand of the one named Keres." Dipaka approached.

"It would seem that you are in need of my help?"

"Yes that's exactly what we are here for."

"Then why have you come only now, am I not worthy to be sought after every day?"

"You are the great Bhoot all of Adelmar has been awaiting your return for some time now!"

The figure moved from his seat and down into the light. "Fear not for I have always been with you!"

"Sankar?" We gasped.

Chapter 8

The temple lit up quickly as the sun drew in upon the first of an elaborate set of light catchers. Sankar tilted one at a time until the entire temple glimmered with hope. The walls were made of gold and layered with a diamond like rock. We followed Sankar on a journey through time as he told us the entire story.

"In the beginning of Adelmar we were one in three Poorvaj, Putra and I, Bhoot. Everything you see in Adelmar was created by Poorvaj and was then placed in the hands of Putra to care for each individual created being. I was the holder of the very spirit of Adelmar until that spirit became corrupted by fear and in the first year of darkness Poorvaj had to leave us to close off Adelmar from any other world."

The paintings on the wall came to life as we walked further into the temple. I leaned into Rutland. "Is it me or does Poorvaj resemble good old Chadwick."

"It was thirty three years of darkness before Putra sacrificed himself to bring the light back to Adelmar. Unfortunately it left the smallest entry way into Adelmar which allowed Kepler to send in his most evil of concoctions, which you know as Keres. She started out a simple organism but grew with great hatred and spread over time to take over almost every part of Adelmar. I believe this is yours." He handed Chadwick peculiar looking pocket watch.

"It is good to see you as well my old friend. I wasn't sure if you were to recognize me." Chadwick took over. "If we are to save Adelmar, Sankar must teach all of you the art of Light Shifting. But first we must eat and find rest."

Dipaka seemingly troubled by all that has unfolded. "So you just went into hiding when your people needed you? Where were you when my parents were taken by Keres or my village burned by her armies? You come back now while we have nothing left!"

"It was the hardest thing I had to do but I could not coincide with darkness or leave my people in the dark. So I gave up my son to light the way for Adelmar once more." Chadwick tried to comfort Dipaka. "My son, my only son died because I couldn't stand being apart from my people. Sankar was sent to be of protection to my people to guide them and to hold off Keres long enough for me to one day return and take back what was rightfully Adelmar's so that none will perish."

Sankar stepped in. "Come Dipaka sit and partake in some of the finest quambee juice you have ever tasted. We must not worry of that which is out of our control."

We sat down for a peaceful meal that left us all a little more enlightened as it were.
"Anyone else feel like we are floating?" Eliza let out a shriek as Holly and I snickered from a distant.

"Best not to look down until you get your head on straight up here." Chadwick gleefully flew by.

"Up where?"

"We are currently sitting over top of the Lamas Mountain range and are higher than the highest point in Adelmar." Sankar Laughed. "The fresh air helps you to clear the mind and free the spirit."

The exhilaration of being so high up left us all a little light headed and Duncan a little more terrified then the rest.

"You have all been granted a circle of light which is currently being controlled by myself and Sankar but in a moment we are going to release control completely into your hands."

"And then!" I gulped. "Rutland can you ask Chadwick to give a little more instruction!" Rutland flew right past me as the rest of us began to free fall back towards the temples roof. "You must learn to compose yourselves and just trust your gut!"

One by one we all landed hard but safe. Dipaka however could not seem to get past his own resentment towards Chadwick and Sankar landing not by his own control but by the guidance of Sankar as Chadwick pulled him into a room right off the main temple.

"Dipaka I know you miss your family deeply and for what it is worth, your family isn't gone forever. I need you to trust me."

"For the longest time I wanted to believe in something bigger than myself. I would see you in fragments when I would be vision casting. One time I looked so hard I saw a day where my family was with me again among the stars."

"You must understand that I had to separate myself from Adelmar as it was the only way to keep the Noti completely safe."

"Why now, why not years ago?"

"All was set in its place from the beginning and all events have their place in time. We need to move forward because in a few short days nothing may be left of Adelmar." Chadwick reached out his hand. "Come we must find your light."

He took Dipaka up one more time as we watched from the courtyard on the backside of the temple.

"Do you think he will do it this time?" Eliza asked Sankar.

"It is tough to say, all depends on how clear his mind is and if he truly opens his heart. I would say he has a fifty percent chance of dying." Sankar laughed as we all looked stunned. "Honestly he cannot fail or we all will fail as the entire group enters, the entire group grows and no one is left behind."

"But then how did the rest of us find the way to land?"

"You only temporarily unlocked the magic within each of you but in order for it to be complete, all must complete the final task." Dipaka and Chadwick came flying in fast. "I don't think they are slowing down, Sankar do something!"

"I am afraid I cannot as Chadwick ordered me to stand down."

We ran towards the landing zone as they flew in faster than the previous time. We hit a force field like energy as we floated off the ground into a suspended state. "Are you seeing this? Arthur your hands!"

We held our hands outwards as we witnessed a tattoo like pattern forming in light on our skin. “Dipaka look at your feet!” As he received the gift of which Sankar spoke highly of.

“I knew you would prove worthy of the call of a Light Walker!” Sankar and Chadwick glanced at one another in the highest of hopes. Chadwick spun around, now clothed in pure white. “Welcome to the ancient society of Light Shifters. For there are no shadows without those to cast light. This is not a title to take lightly as of today Sankar was the last of this magical society. We only have a little time but if we work together we should be able to take back Adelmar from Keres!”

“No time to waste!” Sankar led us into a room marked by a symbol I have seen throughout Rutland’s writings and even in the corner of some of his drawings, it was three lines unmet that left the shape of an unfinished triangle. We entered the room filled with all that Adelmar had to offer. “Please pick out your own light harness.”

As we tried on the bracelet like contraptions each of us finding the perfect fit. Sankar brought Dipaka over a pair designed just for the occasion that a Light Walker was to emerge from the free fall.

“It is believed well, it is truth as you have now all witnessed that Adelmar was born in light and through light all things were made. So it is by light that all things shall change. Travelers from a far will come to salvage that which had been lost, putting into place of pieces that had been fractured by the dark."

"But Chadwick if you created all this, why can you not make it right on your own?" I spoke up.

"I am afraid my dear boy that in order to truly keep our worlds safe, we had to deny ourselves the capability of even thinking of playing god. I am only but one of the wayward travelers here to salvage a world that has my heart and soul."

The rest of the evening was spent unsuccessfully mastering the art of light shifting. I personally felt even worse for Dipaka as light walking was a task I wish upon nobody. The falls were many and the ground harder and harder each time of impact.

"Enough! We will break until morning but truth is morning maybe all the time we have." As the sky changed to a shadowy red, Sankar and Chadwick absconded to a part of the temple off limits to all but the first three."

"Rutland, a word please?" I pulled him aside. "This symbol, I have seen it before." I looked over his body language as he seemed to want to brush it under the rug.

"What about this symbol?" He replied.

"Come on, it's all over your writings and drawings at home and now here? What are the odds? You can tell me Papa… us Sherwood's are excellent secret keepers." I finished with a smirk as I looked at Holly.

"That was low Arthur, low but well played sir." He sat beside me and raised his sleeve to reveal that same marking on his forearm. "Look here, there is more to do with Findas, Adelmar and Hellondal then just creating new worlds for us to adventure. We were sworn protectors of these places and the inhabitants as they were once from our world but needed safe passage during a time where they were being persecuted by plague or by man."

"So you are part of some secret society of protectors that move the oppressed from our world to a place of freedom in another?"

"Take Duncan for instance, he is actually from a tribe of people called the Cherokee. When our people began to settle in the New World, word got back to the brethren that the native people were being destroyed by disease and greed. So we made our way over and began to salvage the tribes into Calestar."

"The Brethren?"

"We operate in secret so that there are only whispers throughout history. We are the Pax Chava which translates roughly to peaceful living."

"I'd say so as it is both Latin and Hebrew, as well as poor grammar."

"The point is we are responsible for all the lives we have salvaged throughout the ages as their lineages have continued in the new worlds we were entrusted with. The Underground Railroad was an honor to be a part of and a sad one at that. Not that anyone would ever truly known that we were apart of it. Unfortunately as long as there have been people and places to conquer there have been Conqueror's and the Conquered. We are the peacemakers, the restorers and the reason that diversity still exists in our world. When famine, war and plague arise we are in the shadows salvaging the little humanity those affected by such atrocities have left."

"Why not just cap off the worlds for good and leave them to their own?"

"Because we are required to salvage and bring back those into our world that civilization thought to be lost forever. So that none shall parish that no people be lost to the darkness of our world completely, all lines of humanity must remain intact."

I took a moment to think through all of history I ever pondered upon before asking my next series of questions that ended with "And the Red Sea splitting?"

"Heavens no, that was a pure act of God." He chuckled. "But from that stemmed what we are today. We are from the line of Moses. It is time for you to take your place beside me son."

He pulled a small ring with a branding iron face in the shape of the symbol of the Pax Chava and sparked it hot to a glow. "Roll up your sleeve, this will only take a second, and done."

My head dizzied off into a slumber that was more complete than most nights. We awoke the next morning to tiny droplets falling from the ceiling, splashing against the rocks above our make shift bedding. "Arthur! Let me sleep just a few more minutes." Eliza nestled into my chest.

"Wakie, Wakie everyone! We have work to do and must not delay! Dipaka you will be training with Chadwick and as for you lot, you all will be with me."

"But Sankar, not even the sun is up!" We grumbled.

"Oh right, yes but unless you all learned to harness your light in your sleep I am afraid we must begin now as we move out before night fall to search for Keres!"

"But what about something to eat?"

He tossed us all some fruit fresh from the temple's orchard. I pulled my arm back in pain.

"You okay Arthur?"

"Yes just tweaked it a bit in my sleep."

"You know Rutland at some point it would be nice to be in a place where someone wasn't always trying to destroy the land and its people." Holly muttered.

"As long as there is land to be had and people to claim it, unfortunately there will always be those who want more even if they have to do unspeakable things to gain such power."

"Why can't we all enjoy it equally and together?"

"Pride, ego, lust, greed… the list goes on and this is why a salvager's job is never truly finished. Ultimately our life is one of restoration, which often comes at a cost of no intrinsic value."

That morning was the most grueling and rigorous process I put my body through in quite some time.

"Of course you will not be able to master the art of light shifting in one day but if I can get you to all work together then we will be able to do just enough to at least hold Keres off from fully destroying Adelmar. And maybe with enough hope and a little luck we may see her vanquished from here forever."

Chadwick entered the room with Dipaka. "You must find the place that gives you most peace and live there."

Rutland leaned over to me. "Chadwick always had the flair for the dramatic. I on the other hand enjoyed the practical side of blending into the world I created." Dipaka then demonstrated as he ran through the air like nothing could hold him down.

My mind flooded with memories of my

sister and I running around the yard pretending we were Knights of the Round Table. I breathed in deeply and for a brief moment I could feel energy surging to my hands.

"Well done Arthur, now transfer it to that flower pot!"

"Arghh!" I let out a loud grunt as the pot exploded into bits and pieces.

"A little less gusto next time!" Chadwick patted me on the shoulder.

Eliza began to lift a small tree as she struggled, Sankar placed a bigger tree on top and shifted both trees directly over top of her.

"Sankar are you insane!"

"Rutland, Arthur… I don't think I can hold it much longer."

"What are you all waiting for, work together, move quickly if you wish to help out your friend!"

Duncan and I quickly flooded our hearts with our fondest memories but Rutland seem to be no use in this matter. "Hold on Eliza!" Duncan and I shifted the two trees slightly higher as Dipaka ran through and pulled her out from under the eventual catastrophe.

The tree splashed hard into the ground being completely decimated into what seemed as though a million pieces. "Rutland? You alright?" He looked particularly disturbed as he couldn't seem to unlock the light we all now possessed.

"It seems that not every secret can be locked away forever." He looked down into the depths of his own soul.

"What more of mystery could there be than me being your son?"

"Arthur what did you say?" Eliza laughed only to realize that it was not a laughing matter.

"Is it true Rutland? Arthur is your son?"

"It is true Chadwick, Arthur is my own flesh and blood as was his sister Cassidy."

"You knew the rules and you broke them! Why didn't you tell me sooner?"

"I was ashamed but also more proud than I ever could have been in my life to have a son and a daughter."

"You knew the repercussions would be on all of us, you knew the cost to creating these worlds."

"I made a mistake but she was the most beautiful woman I had ever laid eyes on!" Rutland pulled out a picture of my mother.

"You didn't make a mistake Rutland! You fell in love, plain and simple, you chose a life we were forbid to have and now we pay the price. And for what? For all we know Kepler could have sent her after you, knowing all the right buttons to push. He only needed you to fail by a speck and you managed to do it by a kilometer." Chadwick scolded.

Rutland looked on as he tossed the photo

into a candle wick and it burned brightly. I could see him pondering the possibility of foul play from Kepler but still he had hoped that all they shared was true love.

"So let me get this straight, the only way those worlds could be yours were if you took an oath to forgo any offspring?"Eve interjected.

"Merlin knew of the game in which we were playing was a dangerous one, so he added a few rules of his own and should any rule be broken it would open up a way for well let's just say the end of our worlds. Rule 1. No one was to ever enter another world. Rule 2. Under no circumstance were we to ever reveal ourselves to the people of these worlds. Rule 3. We vowed to never have children of our own, as this would be our only parental need."

"By my count you have broken them all." Chadwick boasted.

"And it will cost me everything but not before it is restored."

"You were never much for rules." I added.

"Kepler knew the first rule was safe guarded by the memory elixir as well as rule number two for that matter, I guess somewhere along the way he figured out his only way into Findas and Adelmar was for one of us to break rule three knowing full well that he couldn't produce a proper offspring. He decided to send a trusted companion to lure me into a whirlwind type fall fast and break everything kind of love, it would seem."

"You are lying, well not completely." Sankar pushed. "For the truth will set us all free but in this moment it seems nothing has been lifted."

"Well that is not his only secret!" I stepped up. "The truth is quite complicated it would seem. These worlds have been around far longer than Rutland has lead us to believe. Our dear Rutland, Kepler and Von Winkler are part of a secret salvaging society of three in which I was inducted into last night seeing as Kepler in an act of betrayal forwent his place I have taken up his mantle." I held up the marking on my arm.

"Look, the stories are to keep the knowledge of said society at a mere whisper and the important thing to understand is that we cannot let them end on our watch."

"Oh boohoo, let's not wallow about it and move on as it is in a place we can no longer change!" We all looked at Sankar, puzzled. "It is in the relatively distant past!"

"Right you are my good man."

"Sankar do you have the maps of the land on the other side of the mountains?"

"I thought you'd never ask!"

The world of Adelmar opened up like that of an old tale, rivers and hills ran through it most remarkably. It was the change in temperature that truly left me perplexed. The sheer detail of the landscape on the other side of uncharted territory was breathtaking.

"Keres has been held up in a village on the other side of the Jesper River. We must cross in the early morning as the tide and rapids rise faster by the hour, making it most impossible to cross come evening."

Rutland laughed. "You named a river after your dog?"

"It made sense at the time, but none the less that is where we must cross to go undetected. The people of this land are only under her control so let's try to subdue them first and if it is needed but only if you must choose between your own life and their life should you take a life."

"No one is to die today."Rutland stood up assuredly.

Chapter 9

The journey to a most certain death had been all Rutland ever wanted, if you had the chance to look deep enough into his eyes. He walked hand in hand with Eve ahead of us and after have taken an oath of eternal magnitude myself, I understood why he was in need of such rest, and his life lacked any sense of finality for so long. I believe he always meant to pass his place on to me but in light of everything that has transpired maybe having me be a part of the Three is the rest he needed.

"So Sankar what will you do once we free Adelmar from this wicked evil?" I asked.

"I will open up the finest Quambee Juice stand in all of Adelmar and maybe find myself of a companion." He looked elated. "What about you Mister Arthur?"

"I will return home and start a family of my own with this lovely lady." I pulled Eliza closer.

"You will be a great Father, I am sure, but what about the rules you swore to uphold?"

"I may have had my fingers crossed for that third one." We Laughed. "Plus rules to Sherwood's are more like suggestions."

We shared another laugh but honestly given my previous profession Rutland and I may have tweaked the oath for proper safe keeping."

We moved forward about a half days walk before pressing up against our first encounter with a few souls lost to the wicked that is Keres.

As we got closer the colors grew dimmer and the atmosphere darker until the stench of the dying landscape was too much to bare. We wrapped cloths around our mouths and noses to continue pressing onward through the thick air.

"On your right, Chadwick!" Rutland screamed as the wind picked up a trail of darkness flanked us. Sankar took on the first wave without any help of our own.

"Now would be a good time to ready yourselves. This will not be the last of them. Leave here whatever we will not need." Sankar looked shaken but not moved.

We made our way forward into the formation Sankar instructed us to be in. Rutland and Chadwick brought up the rear as Sankar lead the charge along the shadowed hillside.

"Did you tell him everything?" Chadwick whispered to Rutland.

"Only what he needed to hear."

"The immortality stops with us as we cannot let the next in our order get to the same point as Kepler."

"But you see, that is it! Once Kepler separated himself from the oath, he made himself vulnerable."

"You know as well as I the one thing Kepler never was or will be is vulnerable. He calculated every single move he ever made."

"But what he hasn't accounted for is Arthur taking up the oath. When this is all said and done we must part ways and set forth two more to take up our places." Rutland finished right before the ambush.

We fought off one by one the darkness that tried to take over our very souls. The light from our hands fended the wicked warriors of Keres back to a rocky way side where the Light of Adelmar was now gone, we found ourselves face to face with pure evil.

"Run! If you wish to see another day." Sankar led the speeding charge down the back of the hillside as time began to slow within us. The dirt and dust began to explode around us as we made it to some quality covering. "The tall grass of the Brimfield will only protect us a short while."

Chadwick turned around to face the force head on as we turned to make sure everyone made it to the clearing we saw his very last breath as the cloud consumed him and evaporated every particle of his being into the atmosphere. Rutland looked on as a single tear ran down his cheek. Sankar smiled as he watched his oldest friend move on into his greatest calling, finally becoming one with Adelmar.

"I am guessing that was Keres?" We could smell the darkness as it lurked along the field line.

"Duncan come here quickly!" Rutland wiped the tears from his eyes. "Chadwick rightfully named you his successor should he no longer be able to carry on the oath he swore to protect with his life. You as the only remaining person of Calestarian descent is the proper choice. Arthur at the ready."

"Do I have some time to think about this? I have always been a fan of unspecified finality."

"Look this oath no longer carries the weight of immortality as it is not proper for one to hold such a burden. You should name your own heir in your last will and testaments."

"Rutland and I saw that in order to keep the oppressed free from harm that all who are a part of the order of three shall only serve one life cycle. This will protect the past the present and our future as we know it." I explained.

"You must fully understand the oath you are about to take." He looked into Duncan's eyes. "Your people were saved by us as we heard of the travesties going on in the new world as explorers began to settle in the west. Disease and greed almost drove your people to extinction. We exist to save all those under any form of oppression. The lands of what is left shall be yours to protect and to bring all who need your assistance. At my home is a ledger of all missions ever carried out by us to preserve humanity. You now join Arthur and myself as a protector of Pax Chava!"

The moment was short lived as I had some questions of my own. "This ledger you spoke of is where?"

"It is hidden well as I am the only one who knew of its existence for it was mine to keep. I tracked every mission down to the letter including number of those salvaged as well as to where they were relocated. You need only to know that the steps you take matter more than the ladders you should climb."

"Right, more wisdom from the wisest of them all." Holly always managed to add her two cents.

Eliza looked on in approval as she relieved him of his duty as her official Royal Keeper.

Sankar gathered us back up as the stars pushed their way above. "Mr. Chadwick was a great man and it is now because of his sacrifice we stand a fighting chance against Keres before all of Adelmar is consumed."

"What are you going on about?" Eve perked up.

"Keres exposed herself when Chadwick gave up his life. We must move forward and go onto the attack as she was weakened in that moment."

"What about her groundlings?"

"They operate only on the fear of those they prey upon. Please remember that those doing her biddings are unaware of their hand in the matter."

The lot of us spent the next hours fighting our way through the worst of nightmares. Treacherous creatures groundlings were, they moved like smoke along the ground with faceless snake like bodies wrapping us up one by one.

I could hear the water that took my sister from me. I still remember how my father smelled when he scooped me up with tears on my cheeks and anger in my heart. My mother's screeching yell that left us all nearly deaf. Then it took me to the old fields by my house where I would hide and cower until the boys from my neighborhood would leave so that I could survive another day without a beating. I looked up for a split second as I could see the others struggling to make their way through the plain of groundlings. Sankar walking untouched as he slowly freed us one by one. Rutland fell to the ground rolling around. "Fire! I'm on Fire!"

"Rutland, you are ok. There is no fire. It was all in your head."

"Oh thank God. On my short list of fears being burned alive is at the top."

"I never knew the incredible Mr. Rutland Quincy Sherwood to be a man of any fear, let alone you have a list of them."

"It is quite short... being set on fire, frozen to death and having to eat your mothers cooking. I mean your biological mother's cooking, Pip is quite the cook if I might add." Rutland spoke as if Pip was in our midst.

"Love the good old chit chat but we have to keep going. It is only a matter of moments before Keres realizes we made it through the groundlings and are closer to the tree of knowledge." Sankar moved us along.

"So we aren't actually going after Keres?" Dipaka spoke.

"We take out the tree and she has no more power here."

"The tree of knowledge... that is your plan Sankar! You know the temptation that will come of it and you know the consequence if you give in."

"I understand Mr. Rutland it is a great risk that I have been waging the consequences for a very long time."

"Well you will need a lady's touch for sure on this but not everyone need to make the trip. Duncan, myself, Arthur and Eve will make our way with Sankar to the tree for hopefully our last run in with Keres. Dipaka, Holly and Eliza you need to take this map and find your way to the village where I have hidden a passage back to the house inside the elder table."

"I will not leave Arthur!"

"Elizabeth! You will go at once." Eve pushed through. "We need you there for when we finish here and Keres is defeated only then will we return and completely shut the way to Adelmar off until Kepler is defeated and Hellondal is secured."

We embraced for a moment and as Eliza was never one for pleasantries we gave a last look.

"Take these with you and know that to enter through the pass you must shine them over at the ninth hour of the second half day."

"No need to waste time!" Sankar put his arms around the three and in a gasp disappeared only to return in as quickly as he had left.

"You can teleport? And we have been walking this entire time?" I let out a brief moment of disappointment as time was never on our side.

"Well Keres knows we are here already so no need to be sparing with my powers any longer."

"Onto more important things Arthur." Rutland put a light image into the air. "The tree is extremely volatile right now and must always have a care taker. My guess is that Keres was made care taker by Kepler and every day her power grew stronger."

"Stronger I understand by why inherently evil. If the tree is both good and evil?"

"It has long been said that a man and a girl once approached the original care taker in need of nourishment. As the care taker let them into the garden the man struck him down from behind and offered the girl a single piece of fruit from the tree to which bound her to the tree. Though good may still be in her it was the evil she consumed that day that has now consumed her. The man walked away with the only other piece of fruit the tree produced that year."

"Kepler's cane had a gold fruit like knob for a handle." We continued walking.

"The tree has not produced any fruit since that encounter and I am afraid we must burn it to the ground in order to release Keres from his power and render his cane useless."

"Arthur you have a match or two in that

sack of yours?"

"I am afraid Mr. Rutland it is not fire that will burn the tree down but the sacrifice of the willing to bind their heart and restore the garden to its original glory."

Duncan raised his hand. "What are you doing Duncan? The tree will choose only after we separate Keres from its trunk."

"Then we shall let the tree decide on who."

"Whom Mr. Rutland as the Tree needs not one but two to bring it back into balance."

"Well then maybe we should have kept Dipaka and the girls with us." Rutland laughed as Eve swatted him.

For never actually being a dad for but only a short while in admittance, Rutland had the dad humor on lock.

Chapter 10

The soul is a fortunate passenger in those who wish upon nothing but in hope fight for everything that is worth acquiring. For it was this valuable lesson that kept us charging onward as it was the last words written in Rutland's guide. And much like Rutland his writings never said more than they meant and it is why right now in the middle of his journal is the end of all I would need to know about salvaging the impossible.

"Are you still reading my journal?" Rutland

tossed the journal over the edge of the steep incline we traveled by.

"I was but I finished it right where you ended it."

"Well no need to say any more than what needs to be said."

We approached a clearing that led us to a great valley plush with the most bountiful of vegetation. The lushest of colors filled the vast valley.

"The valley is tempting but only light will expose the darkness." At Sankar's ready we sent a surge of light into the void as we saw the ruin that it currently was. Ashes flurrying around the decay leading up to a single tree in the middle with whispers of Keres flying before our ears.

"We must continue with the light as it is the only way to navigate this dreary path of death."

"You will fail her again!" A haunting whisper called out.

"You will never be worthy enough to take her place." It continued on.

"Are you willing to give up your life for one who destroyed all you loved?"

"What will your daughter say? Have you not only just found one another?"

"You are the last of your people oh what a joy it will be to eradicate the last Calestarian."

"Bhoot you old fool. Like father like son."

It was absolute torture that only lasted moments but felt like an eternity as we found our way to the largest tree I have ever seen in my life. Sankar threw the first blow to the base of the tree as we chipped away at the rest of it. Keres began to emerge from within. Duncan and I each grabbed a lock onto her wrists and began to pull as the other three began to cut away more of the tree.

"As soon as she is free from it we must take hold and that which is willing will be selected."

A vacuum like silence exploded into the atmosphere as we completely removed every last part of that evil witch from the sacred Tree. Sankar being the loving man he was split into two and became one with the tree. "Like you said no one else needs to die today."

The color returned to the valley and all of Adelmar was free at once. The ash of Keres began to shift as a hand pushed through the pile a young woman appeared of my resemblence. "Cassidy? Is it really you?"

"I haven't heard that name in ages but of what is it to you and where exactly are we?" She seemed dazed and confused.

"I thought you were dead. I lived with the guilt for so long." I ran to embrace her as Rutland stood their completely perplexed. It was a rare state for him to be found in. "Oh God it is so good to see your face."

Tears filled up the most joyful of reunions as though a part of me always knew or always hoped we would one day see each other again.

Over the next short while we sat by a fire side as we could hear the sounds of revival off in the distance Adelmar was made whole again.

"That day by the waters side when you feared I had drowned a man had pulled me out and by the time I had pulled through I was already under his spell. He told me that if I helped him with one simple task he would not harm Arthur. He brought me to Adelmar for the task at hand was to simply eat a piece a fruit from the tree, but from the moment I took that first bite, I became like a slave to him. I never wanted to hurt anyone I promise."

"I know you didn't Cass."

"How did Mum and Dad hold up?"

"At first Dad was a complete mess and Mum barely went out of the house but there is also something you need to know. Pip and Brunley were more of our guardians as new info has come to light in that Rutland and just like his life a mystery woman are our biological parents."

She sat up with an epiphany. "Yeah that makes total sense. I mean you are a spitting image of Rutland and I always had his fearless care free spirit."

"I should have never let you out of my sight my dearest Cassidy Jane." Rutland held her close.

"Let's not get too sappy now." She nudge him on.

"Right you are child. We have about a day's journey back to the village so we can get home and plan our way to Hellonadal and hopefully restore peace to all lands."

"I fear that I may have been a distraction as Adelmar has been in a deep state of decay since the dark matter took hold of it. Lucky for us while I was under Kepler's control I was privileged to fragments of his grand plan. Our world will see an invasion of a magnitude that it has never seen."

"They wouldn't stand a chance against the technological advances of our societies." I felt confident for a brief moment.

"He isn't simply bringing the people is he?" Cass looked at Rutland.

"No he is going to bring all of Hellondal with him too." Rutland looked into my soul.

"For the Salvagers sake we cannot risk our world being exposed to the others. People returning can be explained but if any of the three worlds was to break into the same dimensional space as ours it would be catastrophic."

"I'm sorry so all of our worlds coexist just on different plains?"

"Yes and last time this almost happened, Calestar was destroyed and Flat Earth believers were born. Which if you ask me they aren't completely insane but to protect the Salvaging Society we just let them run with it."

"Run with it?"

"Well like color blindness, certain people see the world at a frequency that when this anomoly occurs, a world outside of our own time and space collides with ours it goes flat. This anomaly to us goes undetected but to them happens quite often. About three percent of our world population experiences it daily. Out of that three percent only .01 percent can see through the dimensional plains at once. All of which are deemed complete loons and locked in padded white rooms to calm their sense of sight. However few have gone on to change the very way we see our world with music, art, science, mathematics, architecture; the pyramids, the Sistine chapel, Beethoven's 9th, Einstein's theory of relativity..." Rutland rambled on and on. "Sir Isaac Newton... commonly we call them prodigies but for us we know them as the Pioneers."

Rutland always had the inside track on explaining that which seemed separated by instance. He connected the dots leading him all the way around the world and back again. He was never a man short on words.

"The point is we cannot risk exposure for the lives we saved will be lost and the lives that will be needing saving in the future may never have a chance."

"No time to waste then!"

"Anyone have anything to eat. I am famished." Cass put her arm around me. It was odd seeing her again, as she still carried the same smile and laughter about her.

We trekked on throughout most of the afternoon. Adelmar had the same feel of new beginning that we left in Findas. "What is our plan exactly?" Cass spoke up.

"In short, stop Kepler. The how is going to take quite a bit of creativity as he is one for puzzles and if Findas and Adelmar are a sign of what is to come, I expect a total all-out war on our world."

We arrived at the passage Rutland left hidden by a river bed. I had a slightly uneasy feeling as we entered the threshold of Rutland's cellar. "You still have Merlin's Key on you?"

"Of course!"

Moving up the stairs the atmosphere seem to absorb all the sound in the air. We pushed the door at the top of the step open to see Eliza and Holly bound up in the center of the room. Kepler made his grand entrance holding us all with the lower hand. "Out with it!"

"Kepler..." Rutland nodded.

"Out with what?" I had my hands raised.

"Any and all objects that could potentially pose a threat to myself." He demanded.

"You really are pure scum you know that."

"Oh relax Rutty my old boy. You will be dead soon enough."

"You will be!" Cassidy spoke angrily.

"Oh Cassidy my sweetheart. It's been sometime." Kepler winked at her. "Look I will make this simple. Rutland comes with me and no one will get hurt this very moment, however I make no promises of tomorrow."

"Rutland don't do this." I looked him in the eye.

"All journeys must come to an end, my boy."

"How about we shelf this for another time." I smirked as Rutland turned to meet his fate.

"Put these on." Kepler tossed him a pair of restraints. "Now we are going to leave here unhindered or well you get the point."

We moved in quickly to unbind the women. Through the window I could see Kepler making Rutland get into the trunk of his car.

"It took you long enough to get back." Eliza was sharp as ever.

"Cassidy? You are all grown up!" Holly ran to give her a hug.

Cassidy looked confused. "And you are?"

"It's me Holly, your cousin. We use to play dolls and run around the backyard here pretending to be princesses. Your mum and Dad are going to be so happy to see you."

"About that Holly, it would seem that Rutland is our Father." Cassidy thought she was revealing something big.

"Yeah now that you mentioned it. Completely makes all the sense in the world. You barely resembled Pip and Brunley at all." Holly played along as she looked at me with that proud Sherwood smirk. "The way I see it, Aunt Pip and Uncle Brunley will always be your parents as to simply have children is no small task but to raise them up proper is deserving of the title."

"Your sister is alive." Eliza was thrilled for me as we had a moment to ourselves. "Where are Duncan and Eve?"

"They went into Findas with special instructions from Rutland to acquire an artifact or two."

"But they never came back."

"Yeah, Rutland always had more than a way or two in and out of Findas."

"Any idea where Kepler may be off to with Rutland?"

"He was quite keen about a bridge. Never mentioned a name only that it was near the university they taught at."

"Well that leaves only two to pick from but one holds no historical significance what so ever."

"Let's go with that one then shall we." Kepler was a man of little puzzlement, I mean he loved a good puzzle or riddle but when he set out with a goal and the only way to it was from point A to point B. Although he learned a thing or two from Rutland, it was his blind ambition that kept him from seeing the entire picture.

"I know the bridge may not hold any historical secrets but what if the bridge has geographical relevance to Kepler's master plan."

"Wait it would seem that Kepler's father was head architect of this bridge!" Eliza held up a clipping of newspaper that was sitting by the fire place. "Kepler's company was in charge of building a museum to his late father in honor of the anniversary of its completion."

"Oh fantastic another museum. When does it open up to the public?"

"Not for another week but it is said to have exhibits of the likes this world has never seen."

"I bet it does. At this point it is clear that we only have a week to stop him and hopefully Duncan and Eve will be back from Findas to help do so."

With Rutland out of the picture and Cassidy our only link to Kepler's world, it was time to go searching for any and all we could find on the man that Rutland seldom spoke of. We split up as Cassidy and I climbed all the steps leading up to the attic turned archive. Holly and Eliza headed into the thinking room to search behind Merlin's door.

"I remember Rutland's stairs to be a bit

longer." Cass laughed.

"It's funny when you've been away so long how perspectives change, when I hiked up these steps the first time over here since university I barely made it to the top."

Cass flipped one of the pictures on the wall around to my surprise it was one of our drawings we made as children together. "Some things never change. Even in the absence."

"What was Kepler like?"

"Conflicted at first but then as years wore on, the evil grew until no light seemed to be left. As far as being away from all I had ever known, I was well taken care of. He even made sure I kept up with all my studies. Totally jealous of Rutland, if you ask me, I was just a long play in his grand plan. I never felt like he would actually do me any harm I think he just wanted to hurt Rutland but then found a use for me in taking over Adelmar. The man I first encountered was far different from the one we are after now."

We shuffled through stacks of documents and records that Rutland had stored up here from the early days. "Look at this its Kepler with a woman and a child."

"That would be his wife Magdelynn and his daughter Gwyn. One of my care takers told me that they had died shortly after he began working on a secret project."

"Must have been when he started with Rutland and Chadwick."

"He threw himself completely into his work at that point. She even said to some extent it was his own hubris that got them killed. He wasn't completely upfront with Rutland and Chadwick and knew the possible outcome should they find out he took the oath while having a wife and daughter. He hid them for as long as he could but being a part of the salvaging society consumed him so much so that he forgot everything his previous life had to offer until the fateful night when he returned to them to find his house a pile of rubble and ash."

"He tried to destroy Findas with fire and Adelmar with magic. The oath cost him everything and I fear he is now set out to take away everything Rutland ever truly loved."

"She said that it was a few days before I had come to live with them that Kepler went barking mad about something."

"He must have learned who you and I really are or to whom we are."

"Honestly the only thing that kept me alive was his longing for his own daughter."

"Arthur! You need to get down here!"

We walked in to Eve and Duncan back from Findas ready to go to war with all the Keepers at their side. "Well it is good to see you all and I truly am glad you are here but this battle is more so of intellect."

"Rutland asked us to round up the Keepers for he fears we need all the help we can get. I hope you have a plan by now."

"It is an Honor." Hashiro, Akimi, Fergus and Finlay nodded.

"Alright then, Holly we need to get the keepers some more fitting outfits."

She took them to Rutland's everyday clothes closet to find a more suitable appearance as Eliza found Akimi some clothes of her own from her wardrobe.

"Um maybe Fergus should just hold down the fort here and try not to get into too much trouble." As the only thing that would have even come close to fitting him was the bear skin rug in the other room.

"After some thought and research we need to be on high alert and never alone. The museum is set to open tomorrow close to the south side of the bridge. The crowd is said to be in the thousands as the advertisement has made it quite the spectacle."

"Is this Kepler's end game?"

"I fear it is only the beginning to his final plan." He was an avid strategist who had counter moves prepared ten steps out. "Our best chance at beating him is to force him back into Hellondal."

"Arthur and I will head out tonight to do some recognizance work and hopefully get a better idea of what we are up against."

"I am going too." Cassidy stood up. "If Kepler catches you two, you are as good as Rutland right about now. Besides Kepler has a weak spot for me."

We borrowed the car from our lovely neighbor Mrs. Garrison and onward we went with only about seven hours to sunrise and twelve hours until the grand opening.

We parked a few blocks out and pretended to be celebrating our way home from a party.

"The museum entrance should be right up around the corner."

"Let's not get caught shall we."

There were perimeter guards making their rounds like clockwork and a few on the roof. The main entrance and windows were covered up while we could hear the sound of workers hurrying whatever it was they were doing.

"I am going to get a closer look." Eliza said in hushed tone.

It was only a few moments later she returned with a stunned look upon her face.

"What is it? What did you see?"

"Rutland tied to a chair completely beaten and bruised. Blood gushing from his mouth and nose. He doesn't look to be conscious."

"We have to get in there!" Cassidy spoke up.

"We can't risk the entirety of our mission

to satisfy the immediate need."

"But its Rutland!"

"Rutland willingly put himself into Kepler's plan so that we would be spared. We must keep to our plan so that his sacrifice will not stand in vain. Hopefully to save him once more in the process."

"Well then whatever we do, maybe let's put save Rutland at the top of the list. All I have of my father is a few harrowing jealous tales Kepler use to ramble on about."

"I'll be right back!" Eliza made her way into where Rutland was being held.

"Let's get out of here, he is awake but he wasn't mobile." Eliza hurried out with a program from the coming events and few press passes.

"Did you see anything else in there?"

"Loads of exhibits with nothing currently in them, just glass fronts and large empty spac-es."

"Empty exhibits doesn't make any sense. The public will be outraged."

We pulled up to the house and tried to get what rest we could manage for the fate the world hangs in a delicate unknown balance at the hand of complete lunatic who is now given a prop-er motive as he lost everything and a man with nothing to lose is more dangerous than a man with the world to gain.

Chapter 11

The morning entered the windows with a glaring sense of hope as we prepared to make our way down to the museum in staggered groups as to not draw any unwanted attention. I felt the weight of four worlds upon my heart with every step we made on our way to the grand opening.

The London air was dense with anticipation and the excitement was palpable. It was in that dense atmosphere I could hear an all too familiar voice.

"Arthur! Eliza! What on earth are you doing back so soon?"

"What are your parents doing here? I mean

what are Brunley and Pip doing… oh look they brought the entire family along too." Eliza loved pointing out the obvious.

"Mum… Dad what on earth are you doing here?"

"We were given special invites on behalf of the Kepler Foundation. He was one of Rutland's oldest friends. We would have invited you as well but we thought you were…"

"Well we are back. Dad a word?" I pulled him aside on the crowded walkway.

"How was holiday?"

"I will tell you all about it later. By the way when was it you were planning to tell us that Rutland was our father?"

"What do you mean us and who told you? I bet it was Auntie Rose."

"Oh right." In my own excitement I forgot that he was unaware of the current family affairs so I switched back to the issue at hand. " Rut-land's old friend Kepler."

"Yeah he is having an exhibit dedicated to Rutland. That is why the entire family is here. To see it before the public is allowed in. We are guests of honor." He held out his invite proudly.

"I wouldn't call him a friend and I said us because if you look over there across the street the young lady with a strikingly Sherwood appearance is Cassidy, She is alive dad but we cannot blow her cover."

"That's not possible."

"He figured out who Cass and I really were to Rutland and kidnapped her. He isn't who he appears to be. You need to get the family out of here."

"Umm I would but they are heading into the exhibit with your wife at this moment." They made their way into a special entrance.

"Well looks like you will be filling in for Eliza then. Just stay with me. Oh and so that there is no more surprises. Rutland faked his own death and Kepler is currently holding him captive, you might want to cut Auntie Rose some slack as it was Rutland who came clean to me and also I will give you the short story is if we do not stop Kepler from his plan which as of now we are only grasping at straws to what he is up to. The fate of our world is at hand and Rutland did a bit more than just salvage artifacts in his day." The look on his face trying to process everything was that of my mother's when she knew something before I even said it.

"If I have taught you nothing is that Sherwood's always stick together and you pretend like you are the first Sherwood, Rutland tried to get into the family business. Who do you think bailed Rutland out of all of his misfortunate business dealings and legal issues on the better half of his life?" He rolled up his sleeves.

"You think Rutland would trust the upbringing of his children to anyone? He and I have a few secrets of our very own, I have you know. You didn't think I recognized Eve at your wedding?" Now I had that same look of processing on my face as it just hit me that Rutland always had an outside man.

"Well look we need to get to Kepler before he has a chance to do what we believe will be his final play to bring down all Rutland gave his entire life to protect."

"Well what's your plan to get all of these people out of here?"

"Kepler clearly wanted to have the upper hand and now he does as our entire family is in there. I fear our only option is a simple one. Pull the fire alarm."

"A bit of a problem as there will be a guard at almost every alarm post."

"Plus knowing Kepler he will have his most trusted men walking around as guests."

"Let's light the place on fire then?"

"Maybe not the entire place. How about just a trashcan in the loo will do?"

As the general public made their way past the ticket gates we made our way into the first available lavatory. "Stuff as much toilet paper into the trash receptacle and leave a little trailing so we can get some distance." The paper torched faster than anticipated.

"That should do it Arthur."

"Fire!" I yelled as we stepped into the corridor. "Fire! Please make your way to the nearest exit."

The people scurried on out in an orderly fashion as we made our way to the exhibit said to be honoring the pioneer himself The Incredible Mr. Rutland Quincy Sherwood. We took a quick peak behind the curtain to see Rutland in the center of the room tied to a chair as there were very life like mannequins on different exploits strung throughout the room. There was no sign of the rest of the family until Brunley pointed me to the observation deck where they were looking on with intrigue from behind some oddly thick glass.

"Welcome to the wonderful world of lies of the mildly entertaining sideshow of Rutland Quincy Sherwood the con-artist himself, has graced us with his presence today for a show you will all enjoy." Kepler made his way to the center of the room.

"Arthur I hope you have more than just us here to thwart him." We turned around to see at least a dozen of Kepler's associates heading our way.

"You thought he was Incredible." Kepler continued on. "I am afraid this is his end. It was a good run."

Cassidy, Duncan, Holly and the Keepers stormed into the back of the exhibit. Brunley engaged in an all-out brawl in the hallway.

"This is going to hurt in the morning." Brunley laughed as he sent the first foe through the sculpture leading into the exhibit. I looked on in amazement as it finally dawned on me that maybe Brunley's warning was one from experience in regard to things that involved Rutland.

"Heads up." I tossed a shattered piece of the statue through the shoulder of one of Kepler's men pinning him to the door as Brunley ducked. He looked stunned as we finished off the rest of the combatants and entered the exhibit.

"Nooooooo! Arthur it's a trap!" The doors locked behind us. Rutland and Evelyn were trapped behind one glass enclosure as our entire family was trapped behind another.

"You can either save Rutland and Eve or your entire family. Either way their deaths will be on your conscious."

"Cassidy my sweet Cassidy!"

"Dad!" She gave Brunley a huge hug filled with tears of reunion.

"Everyone alright?" I leaned into the center of the room.

"We will live, a little bruised but never broken."

The tanks started to fill with water as we began to think our way through every possible option. I tapped the glass as it was too solid to just break.

"Kepler is just buying time. For his next move. If he didn't need Rutland well then Rutland would already be dead. Killing us in public would put him in a bind but however keeping us locked up is maybe what he intended this entire time."

"How come no one is panicking?"

"That's because the rooms are not really filling up with water it's an optical illusion. To keep us from figuring out a way out of this room." Holly pointed to the light hitting the glass. "He is using some sort of projector system. I've only seen at the university."

Maybe she had learned a thing or two at university after all.

"Stand back." Duncan pulled a little sphere out of his pocket. "You may wish to cover your ears."

With a poof and a sizzle the glass crumbled to the ground but Rutland and Eve were nowhere to be found. However on the other hand my entire family stormed us with questions that I felt were best left to my dad. "Brunley mind giving them a tour of the rest of the museum."

The rest of the Keepers doubled back to the house as Cassidy shared an unexplainable heart felt moment with my mum. Truth be told mom always felt as though Cassidy was still out there.

"Eliza we need to head to our next appointment." I nodded our way out of the predicament.

"We will see you all at next weekend's family gathering."

We made our way out to the car through the endless crowds. "What do you think Kepler's next move is?"

"He needs both Eve and Rutland. My bet is that they are heading back to where it all started."

"The Church?"

"No that is only where it started for the three of them but for Rutland it started at..."

"The abandon factory off Elm?"

"Precisely! He must have started them at the church and as soon as he felt it was necessary brought them into the factory." I pulled out the photo of Kepler, Rutland, and Von Winkler out of my pocket. We drove as fast as we could as to not raise suspicion. We pulled up to the factory gate that had been left open with a rusty chain dangling off the latch.

"This way." I grabbed her hand as we made our way to the side of the factory.

"Been here before have you?"

"My mates and I use to run around here when my parents would let me stay with Rutland for summer leave. Hopefully the fire escape is still in working order."

The lights were on as we peaked through the window we could see only Rutland chained up as a woman approached him from behind in the shadows to remove his blindfold. "That must be the lady Kepler sent after Rutland."

"Wouldn't that make her your mother?"

"It didn't dawn on me actually."

"Can you hear what they are saying?"

Kepler walked into the room. "You will give us what we need or this will be a long night?" He screamed as the woman left the room.

"Whatever it is you seek? I assure you that you won't find it with me."

"It is very simple! Give me the way back into Adelmar as I already know that is where you have hidden the capsule that will unite all of our worlds and I let you live for now."

"There is no way back! The way was shut when Von Winkler died."

"I know there is nothing more I can do to you. So my lovely assistant will have to take it out on the only thing you have to love." Sounds of torture came from the other room as we could no longer sit back for our chance to save the day.

"Alright! Go to where I was buried and you will find a second plot. Remove the tomb and plunder the lot."

"See I told you he would give it up for me."

"Eve? You..." Rutland didn't look as surprised as us when we broke into the factory floor.

"Mum what are you doing?" Eliza demanded.

"My darling Eliza, come over here and

meet the true king of Findas. Your father and I will need you to join us now."

"You betrayed us but why? You told me dad was dead."

"I told you she wouldn't come with us. She clearly is with them."

"With them? But you betrayed our very world. You sent me away and expect me to just go with you and turn my back on my husband and Rutland?"

"Betrayal? Is only for those who actually had genuine love for those they hurt in the first place." Rutland scoffed.

"Oh pipe down you old fool. Findas only suffered a minimal loss in comparison to what we did to the real Kepler and Hellondal. It was quite easy to be honest, faking the king's death at the hands of an old friend."

"Agnar killed the king and Kepler was just using Agnar to rule Findas." Rutland started to spin his wheels.

"Agnar was our best friend growing up and played the villain role quite nicely for us. When we realized that your friend Kepler had sent Agnar into our world with such a small vision. We three paired up and plotted our escape. We spotted you quite a few times in Findas before we hoodwinked you into believing the king was murdered and I was in need of saving. You fell head over heels for me thanks to my adorable daughter who I begged you to take back with you."

"Your husband followed me did he?"

"Next up, we tried to reason with your pal Kepler only to find him a bit annoying for our liking. So we made him disappear and the hardest part was making everyone believe my husband to be Dietrich Kepler. We had some forced cooperation from Merlis and a potion or two later he was Kepler." She smirked at her achievement fiendishly.

"You really are just pure evil." Rutland said in disgust.

"Adelmar is about to receive the same fate as Hellondal and it is all for the good of Findas. You see these Salvagers bring more and more people into our worlds forgetting to fix the actual evil in this world. So after we finish what we started in Adelmar. We will bring earth back to the dust from which it came."

"We simply won't let you do that?" I stepped forward.

"Let us?" Eve stabbed Rutland deep in his abdomen and dumped him on us as she and well the Kepler imposter as it were made their way to the exit.

"Rutland!" He was covered in blood as he laid in my arms Eliza wiped the sweat and exhaustion from his face.

"I am afraid this is it my dear Arthur. You

and your band of misfits are now in charge."

"This cannot be how you leave us. No exuberant finale."

"I am leaving this world the way I had hoped for."

"But my mother betrayed you, she and my father are the reason you are…"

"At peace. They are how I know the love of my life was real. That it was Eve who was to destroy me." He started to wince.

"Easy now Rutland." He sat up a bit.

"It is also how I know that your mother, well biological mother is safe and sound."

"Right and that is because?"

"Evil is not such a simple endeavor as some may have seen the light and still choose to do that which is wrong. While others never fully emerge from the darkness they were born into. Either way my dearest loves we must never lose sight of redemption as that is the foundation of the Salvaging code."

"Is really now the best time for another Rutland exposition?" I quipped and he continued.

"Though we have found ourselves in a place to bring hope and restoration to those we have been called to, never forget that we too were one time or another in desperate need of that same light and salvaging ourselves. Never perfect, Always better!"

"Alright you, now conserve your breathing."

"Arthur you must have Cassidy take up my oath." He continued with more labored breathing.

"You got it. Done." I quickly agreed to get him to quiet himself.

"It is time that the brethren be more than a club of misfit boys but rather could use a woman's looking after." Rutland struggled with his breathing as he coughed up some blood.

"What is important now is..." I tried again as he cut me right off.

"The most important things in life are never buried. I'm sorry Felicity." He looked up at us as the final glimpse of light left his mortal body.

"Felicity?" I puzzled.

Eliza burst into tears as we had to leave him for now and chase down her parents. I reached into his shirt pocket as he was well known to carry a pocket square or two if the occasion ever required it. I unfolded it to wipe the tears from her eyes. Hand stitched in the corner read. "Love your sweet Felicity."

She looked me in the eyes with a look I've seen only once before. "I am going to end this tonight. There will be no more talking."

"Shall we go and head them off at the plot." To understand what Rutland truly said was to know that he never planned on dying in the first place and so he was never actually buried however he did own a cemetery and the second plot was where he kept a few of his more valuable pieces.

We pulled into the eerie rundown entrance at the top of the hill and began to trek the way to the place he spoke of, with us both on high alert.

"Dig over here." We could hear Eve sputtering about.

"You killed him!" Eliza ran towards Eve as they began to fight most ferociously.

"I wouldn't do that if I were you!" I held her father off from getting involved with a little encouragement from Rutland's pistol he carried in his ankle holster.

"Yes I did kill him and I would do it again. Don't you see how we could rule not just in Findas but here and Adelmar and Hellondal as well?"

"For what more power? Haven't enough people died in your pursuit for total power? What about all those lessons you taught me?"

"It was a con my dear. Just keeping up the appearance until it was time to strike. One day you will understand why I did all of this for you."

"You did none of this for me. You just tell yourself that to help you sleep at night."

"You ungrateful child." They continued on fighting until Eliza lost her footing and I could no longer stay out of it as she was hanging on for dear life on the edge of the steep incline Eve went to make her escape as they found the one off passage way back into Adelmar. "Next time you won't be so lucky my child."

I pulled her up as she found her feet to pull one of her last throwing daggers from her neatly pulled back hair. "You were no mother to me."

Eve moved ever so slightly out of the way as the dagger flew past her eyes and into the heart of the only one she ever loved outside of herself. Cold as ice she looked back at Eliza. "You will pay for that. Not now but your life will be mine to take." She disappeared leaving the lifeless body of her love to rot in a world he only briefly knew.

"You alright Love?"I looked over at Eliza.

"Yeah I'll be all sorted out soon enough."

We dusted ourselves off made our way to the car and about half way home we remembered we must go back for Rutland's body.

"Should we prop him up in the back or just put him in the trunk?"

"Maybe just lay him in the back." With Rutland in tow, we somberly made our way back to the house where we were greeted by not only the Keepers but by every member of the Sherwood family. "Best leave Rutland in the car."

I approached Brunley first to make him aware of everything and he made sure that no one else was the wiser. Eliza stormed past everyone as she needed a moment to decompress.

"Please forgive her everyone, my wife is a

bit under the weather."

"I bet she is pregnant she is."

"No, no just needs some peace and quiet is all." After they didn't get the hint my Mum and Dad stepped in to bid everyone farewell as it was getting late.

"We will see you all on Sunday for some good cheer and plenty of food." I closed the door and without as a bit of a moment I had to debrief every one of our current circumstance.

"What do you mean Kepler isn't really Kepler?"

"The King and Queen of Findas fooled us all."

"The Queen is a traitor?"

"She is a trader and maybe even more motivated now as she has been exposed and her partner eliminated."

"Eliza killed her own father?"

"Correct. Lets not dwell on the parental titles. She really threw the dagger at her mum anyways."

"Hellondal is in peril?"

"It may not exist at all. After they killed the real Kepler no one was left to tend to it and it began to decay into a wasteland."

"The Queen is stuck in Adelmar?"

"For now. There is no way in for us but also no way out for her as Rutland closed them all off. Our only hope is that she plays nice with the people of Adelmar until we can find a proper solution. We must take care of Findas for now and figure out how to get into Hellondal to begin the restoration process. We must stay on high alert but go back to our daily routines until Eve shows herself."

"Our mother I mean Rutland's wife is still alive?"

"It was true love for them." I handed Cassidy the matching handkerchief from Rutland's pocket.

"And Rutland?"

"The incredible Mr. Rutland Quincy Sherwood has succumbed to life's greatest journey, death."

For he never saw death as an end but an infinite beginning. And with that we got Rutland out of the car to have some proper shenanigans before putting him in his favorite outfit from his favorite picture. We then made our way to the back yard where we once dug a hole that had no need to fill but now we stood over the not particularly lifeless body of the most unique man who ever lived.

"In life and in death, he greeted both with humility and curiosity. For today we say not goodbye to a fellow traveler but to a man who put the needs of everyone even his foes above his very own. He loved fiercely. He gave up the simple joys of day to day living in order to go and restore the simple livings of those who called upon his services. He lived a true life of finders, keepers; as he would say that the greatest keep of all is the love you share with one another." I looked down for a moment as I could hear him saying to me time and time again.

"Never perfect my dear boy but always better."

"He would tell me that a life truly lived is one that will never be perfect but we must always be better. Solve one small problem a day and the big picture will come into focus. To Rutland!"

We raised a glass to a man who, poured his empty, for the betterment of humanity long ago. I gripped the key and arrow in my pocket and smiled as not everything had to be extraordinary in purpose but somethings were just a simple reminder of our greater purpose. Tears were necessary but the laughter and smiles and warmth we all felt was more powerful than any sorrow we could ever share. Cass handed me the extra pocket square back as we made our way into the house I noticed the corner had some loose stiches to which I peeled back to see the name Felicity Reed 12 Grimborrow Way and on the other side a poem in Rutlands handwriting.

"Though not under lock and key
My love for you has kept you from me
And in secret I must keep
And in secret I must find

My way back to you one breadcrumb at a time"

I looked at the handkerchief knowing exactly where the breadcrumb trail started and shook my head as I realized that though he asked me to call him incredible as being someone who has now stood where he stood and took the oath that he took. I can say with no qualms that in life he was to everyone else incredible as the stories of his life are most certainly tall ones at that but he is most undoubtedly to me the credible Mr. Rutland Quincy Sherwood and that he is.

To my loving Father who could make the simplest of incidents into the grandest of tales. To my loving mother who was the voice of every bed time story I had ever heard. To my Brothers and their wives who have brought joy and wonder to this world by making me an uncle many times over. To my Sons, may your adventures be worth writing about. To my Loving wife who has given me the gift of both deep friendship and fatherhood, I adore you all.

- Daniel

To the readers, fellow adventurers and fans of The Finder's Keep Trilogy. The past five years of writing has been a passion project, a companion of sorts and at the start an exercize in imagination as I worked through my own struggles with the side of life that exists in our minds. Thank you for your curiousity. Cheers!

-Never Perfect. Always Better, D.A. Reed